The Chancery Lane Conspiracy

Joan Lingard

The Chancery Lane Conspiracy

Catnip

CATNIP BOOKS
Published by Catnip Publishing Ltd.
Quality Court, off Chancery Lane
London
WC2A 1HR

First published 2010

3 5 7 9 10 8 6 4 2

Cover design by Claire Bond
Cover illustration by Lindsay Ellis Coils

A CIP catalogue record for this book is available from the British Library.

ISBN 978-1-84647-108-7

Printed in Poland

www.catnippublishing.co.uk

For Söti and Stella

Contents

Chapter One:
Joe's Big Day

It was the first of January, 1901, exactly a year to the day since Elfie had been taken as an orphan from the streets of London and brought to the *Pig and Whistle* by Constable O'Dowd.

Elfie always found the start of a brand new year exciting. You never knew what might happen. Everyone was talking about Queen Victoria, who was eighty-one years old and ailing ("on her last legs" as Ma Bigsby put it) and not expected to last long. When Elfie had asked how many pairs of legs you could get altogether Ma had told her not to be cheeky. Pa Bigsby said they'd have a new king on the throne before the year was out. A new king!

But today was Joe's big day.

Elfie jumped out of bed. Somersaulted almost, knocking into Ivy's bed. Six girls slept in the room so the mattresses almost touched.

'Wotcha doin'?' grumbled Ivy, turning over. 'It's the middle of the night.'

Elfie ignored her and lit the gas lamp. Ivy was always grumbling. The light flickered over the faces of the other girls: fifteen-year-old Mabel, the eldest, who lay on her back snoring slightly, the eight-year-old twins Nancy and Dora, curled up together, and Vicky, who had just turned five. Cuddles, the youngest of all the orphans, slept in Ma and Pa Bigsby's room.

Elfie could hear someone stirring in the boys' room across the landing. That would be Joe, getting himself dressed up like a toff. She grinned. He didn't like the clothes, but he'd have to wear them. He said his arms and legs felt stiff as if they were encased in armour. Joe liked to run free through the streets. He had long legs and could run like a whippet. Elfie poured some water from the pitcher on the dresser into the china basin and sloshed it over her hands and face. Then she dried herself and dressed quickly, putting on her best red velvet dress with its newly washed white lace collar.

'Get up!' she ordered, yanking the covers back from each of the other girls in turn. 'You don't want to miss Joe leaving, do you?'

'He's only goin' away for the day,' complained Ivy, still grouchy. 'You'd think he were goin' to 'Merica.' She sat up. 'And what are you all dressed up for?'

'I'm going with him,' retorted Elfie, as she tugged a brush through her wild dark curls.

'That ain't fair,' cried Ivy. 'Why should you get to miss school?'

But Elfie wasn't listening. She was on her way down the stairs, leaping over three at a time.

'Mind you don't break your neck,' called Ma Bigsby, who could see her through the open kitchen doorway. 'Or dirty your clean white stockings, as well you might, if I know you.'

Ma Bigsby, a large canvas apron wrapped around her stout middle, was stirring a huge cauldron of porridge on the stove. She had eleven orphans to feed although Elfie could no longer be classed as a proper orphan for she'd found her father a few months back. Once she had come to know him she'd got fonder and fonder of him but she hadn't wanted to go and live with his family. She already had one at the *Pig and Whistle*. Instead, she'd opted to stay here during the week and visit her father on Sundays. There was too much going on at the *Pig*, especially Saturday night sing-songs in the bar. There was never any rowdiness or drunkenness, though. Ma ran a well-ordered public house and didn't put up with any nonsense.

'You could stir this porridge for me while I cut the bread,' said Ma. 'But mind you don't dirty your dress. Put a pinny on.'

Elfie hummed while she stirred the thick grey porridge. Mabel came in with Cuddles and the other young ones, Albert, Vicky and Sam, and seated them at the table. Mabel was never ruffled and could get them to do what she wanted without a fuss. Everyone was fond of her. That was why Ma had let her stay on. Normally the orphans, once they were fifteen, left to go out and make their way in the world. Then there would be room for another. There never used to be more than ten orphans in the house at a time. That was before Elfie had arrived to become the eleventh.

Billy was next to appear. At thirteen, he was a year older than Elfie and Ivy, and one younger than Joe, who was the eldest of the five boys. Ma asked Billy to stoke up the stove. Everyone had jobs to do. In a household of thirteen there was no lack of work.

Ivy slid in to take her seat. She stuck her tongue out at Elfie when Ma's back was turned. Elfie retaliated.

They were only waiting now for Pa Bigsby and Joe.

They arrived together, Pa in his lavender-coloured suit, with his flowing white hair neatly brushed and Joe in a cracklingly new black suit, white shirt and stiff, upright, winged collar. He didn't look at all comfortable. He was trying to tug the collar away from his neck with his forefinger.

'My,' declared Ma, 'if you don't look like a right gent, Joe!'

'He looks like he's goin' to a funeral,' giggled Ivy.

Elfie glared at her. 'He's going to be a lawyer!'

'I'm not, Elfie,' he said quietly.

'You will be one day.'

'I'm going to be an office boy.'

'We've all got to start somewhere,' said Ma.

'Mrs Crabbit,' put in Ivy, 'her wot 'elps out at the grocer's, says a boy like Joe ain't got a chance in 'ell to get to be a lawyer.'

'And why should he not, Ivy?' demanded Pa Bigsby, as he took his seat and tucked his napkin in at the neck so that it covered his front. 'And please remember you should say "hasn't" not "ain't". Nor is there such a word as "wot". Really, your grammar is getting worse!' He was their teacher and a stickler for grammar. He looked directly at Ivy. 'I shall assume "'ell" doesn't mean what I think it does. Well? You haven't answered my question.'

Ivy didn't dare answer. She looked down at her plate but Elfie saw she was still simmering.

Pa Bigsby said Grace. 'For what we are about to receive may the Lord make us truly thankful.'

Joe ate very little. Only a spoonful or two, Elfie noticed. Ma didn't say anything, not this morning, although usually she made them clear their plates. She didn't tolerate waste. She'd tell them some kids were starving on the streets of London. Elfie knew all about that. She'd been one herself.

After she'd finished her porridge Ivy gathered sufficient strength to defend herself. 'Pa, it ain't my fault wot Mrs Crabbit says.'

'Isn't. I agree, Ivy, it is not. But you do not have to repeat it. A woman like Mrs Crabbit is mean-minded. In this household we do not like mean minds.'

That silenced Ivy, for the time being.

They were still seated at the table when the door

blew open and in came Florrie, their barmaid, her long earrings birling. Elfie loved those earrings, the way they spun and glinted in the light. She was determined to get a pair as soon as she was old enough.

Florrie didn't usually come in until later in the morning but she'd wanted to wish Joe luck.

'You look like a real gent, Joe!' she said, echoing Ma. 'Stand up till I see you proper like.'

Elfie wondered that Pa Bigsby didn't ever correct Florrie's grammar. He didn't correct Ma's either.

'Come on, Joe!' urged Florrie.

Joe got up, unwillingly, keeping his eyes down.

'Turn around till I get a good look!'

He turned.

Next to arrive was Constable O'Dowd, Florrie's sweetheart, known to them all as Dowdy. The two of them were saving up to get married and the girls were going to be bridesmaids. Elfie couldn't wait for the day! She wished they'd hurry up and get on with it.

Dowdy whistled at the sight of Joe. 'I wouldn't have knowed you, lad, if we'd passed in the street.'

That was daft, thought Elfie. You'd know Joe anywhere. How could you not?

'Time to get cracking or you'll miss the bus!' Ma had her eyes on the big wall clock. The hands stood at fifteen minutes before eight. Their bus was due at two minutes past the hour. 'Go and clean your teeth, Joe. You, too, Elfie!'

Elfie scrambled up the stairs, gave her teeth a quick

swipe with the toothbrush and then fetched her blue velvet cloak from the big wardrobe on the landing. She loved the cloak with its cosy hood lined with white fur. Her father had bought it for her.

She returned breathless to the kitchen. Joe was there already, being helped into a black overcoat by Pa Bigsby. He was protesting that he didn't need a coat, as he never normally wore one, nor a hat either. A bowler hat.

'This day, Joe,' said Pa, 'is not normal. It is special.'

'Don't forget his brolly!' cried Ma. 'It's there, beside the cupboard.'

Pa handed over the long black umbrella and Joe's big brown eyes goggled.

'All the city gents carry brollies,' said Ma firmly. 'Get your cloak on then, Elfie. You'd best take a brolly and all. It might well rain. It were spittin' earlier.'

Elfie swept the cloak around her shoulders.

Ma frowned. 'Stay still a moment, girl.' She moved closer to Elfie and bent her head to get a better look. 'You got a greasy mark on the velvet. How did that happen?'

'There can't be!' But Ma was right. 'That weren't there before.'

'Wasn't,' said Pa.

'It wasn't! I know it wasn't. I put it away carefully. I'd have seen it. Somebody's done that deliberately!' Elfie looked over at Ivy.

'What you starin' at me fer?' asked Ivy. 'I never touched your stupid old cloak.'

Elfie knew that she had. She could see it in her eyes.

'You cannot make accusations without evidence, Elfie,' said Pa. 'I am sure no one here would do such a thing.'

Elfie felt like crying, or screaming. Probably screaming. 'It's ruined my cloak!'

'No, it hasn't.' Ma held out her hand. 'Give it here. I'll dab it with a bit of hot water.'

She did her best but you could still see that the velvet had been marked. They said looks could kill. Elfie wished they really could. If so, she'd do Ivy in right now. She supposed Pa Bigsby would call that mean-minded. It was just as well he couldn't see inside her head, though sometimes she thought he could.

'Let's get on our way then!' he said briskly.

Ma held Elfie back for a moment. 'You and Ivy'll have to stop this sparring. We can't have it going on in the house. It gives me a right headache so it does.'

'I hate her! And she hates me. She's jealous.'

'You're a luckier girl than she is, you've got to remember that. You found your father.'

'None of the others have. And they don't hate me.'

'But Ivy had a mum and father and they didn't want her.'

Elfie wasn't surprised.

'That made it worse, you see. All the other orphans came here because their parents were dead. Makes a difference. Knowing your parents would have kept you if they could. Your mum would have done if she'd lived.

'So I want you to make an effort to get on with Ivy,' Ma concluded. 'I don't expect you to be best friends, just to get on.'

Best friends! With Ivy! That would take some doing. Joe was her best friend.

'Elfie,' called Florrie from the hall. 'You're going to miss the bus!'

Elfie ran. The others were already out on the pavement, lined up at the stop. The street was busy at this time of the morning. Carts rattled past, two, three, four in a row, their backs loaded up with logs and bags of coal and sacks of potatoes. The drivers cracked their whips, urging the horses on. Some of the animals looked as if they were on their last legs, like Old Queen Vicky. Pa would tick Elfie off if she were to call their Queen that out loud. He would say it was disrespectful. He used words like that. Billy waved to one of the drivers as he went by. The man sometimes gave Billy a lift down to King's Cross station. Billy was mad about trains. Pa Bigsby was going to try to get him a job on the railway when he turned fourteen.

Elfie leaned out to get a better view. A carriage was approaching, moving more smoothly than the carts. A stuck-up looking lady in the back was wearing half a dead bird on her wide-brimmed hat. She gave them a scathing look as she swept past. Little did she know that Joe was on his way to Chancery Lane of all places!

'It's coming!' cried Elfie, as she spotted the dark green bus. The No. 49 would take them as far as Islington where they would change on to the 89.

The three horses came clopping in towards the stop, the breath from their nostrils turning to white steam in the cold morning air.

'Whoa!' cried the driver.

The horses pulled up and stood pawing the ground, their flanks quivering. The bus looked full. Faces pressed against the windows.

'Cor blimey,' cried the conductor, when he saw them all. 'There ain't room for the lot of you.' Then he noticed Constable O'Dowd. 'Got a bit of trouble on your hands, have you, Constable?'

'Trouble?' said Dowdy. 'Not a bit of it. I'm here to see my two young friends off.'

'Don't worry, sir,' put in Pa Bigsby, 'for we do not all wish to travel.' He had donned his top hat and was carrying his silver-topped cane. 'Only two of our number.'

'Just as well. There'll be room up top then if they don't mind getting their heads blowed off.'

Elfie and Joe preferred to ride on the top deck, no matter what the weather.

'Got your coming-home money put away safe and sound now, Elfie?' asked Ma.

'It's in my pocket.'

'Keep hold of it. Your brolly too. They don't grow on trees, you know!'

'And don't be away too long,' added Pa. 'As soon as Joe is settled I want you back here for your lessons.'

'Can I not just stay a little while?' pleaded Elfie.

'Absolutely not! We shall be studying algebra later on this morning. It is not your best subject.'

Algebra! Elfie couldn't make head nor tail of it. She liked history and English best. Once she'd learned to read she'd come to enjoy books, especially adventure stories. Sometimes at the end of morning school Pa Bigsby would read to the older children the mystery stories from *The Adventures of Sherlock Holmes* by Arthur Conan Doyle. They'd just finished one called 'The Five Orange Pips' and were about to start on 'The Adventure of the Speckled Band'. Whilst she didn't mind missing algebra she wouldn't want to pass up the chance of a story.

The driver was getting annoyed. 'Come on, then, if you're coming! Or I'll be running late.'

Pa moved the queue back to allow Elfie and Joe to go forward. The conductor gave Joe a long look as he stepped on board and scrutinised the pennies he handed over for their tickets.

'They're *real*,' hissed Elfie. 'They ain't counterfeit.'

'Elfie!' Joe shook his head at her.

Well, what a cheek the man had treating them like that, as if they might have stolen the money or minted it themselves! He glared at Elfie but passed over their tickets. Then he raised his hand and pulled the bell.

'Good luck, Joe!' cried everyone.

'Yes,' said Pa Bigsby, raising his cane, 'the very best of luck, Joe lad!'

Elfie and Joe scrambled up to the top deck and found that the two front seats were vacant. The bus shuddered as it began to move. The residents of the *Pig and Whistle* stood on the pavement waving and Elfie and Joe hung over the rail to wave back. The pub's sign that hung above the door swayed in the wind, making it seem as if the pig and his whistle were dancing. Elfie laughed. A last wave and they turned a corner. They were on their way.

Joe took off his hat.

Chapter Two:
Chancery Lane

The No. 89 bus from Islington was red. Elfie loved the different colours of the London buses. They came in all shades: light blue, dark blue, blue and white, light green, yellow, chocolate, orange. She liked the yellow ones best. They glowed in the dusk. It wasn't often that she got the chance to ride on any of them. When she went to her father's house on Sundays he collected her in his motor car. That was exciting and all the kids envied her. Sometimes he'd give them a ride up to the park and back as a treat. But for Elfie the top deck of the bus was a treat.

'Plenty of room up there,' the conductor told them. He was much nicer than the previous one.

They got the seats at the front again. Nobody else seemed to want them.

'Well,' said Elfie, as they settled themselves, 'ain't this exciting?'

'Isn't,' said Joe and laughed.

Elfie was glad to hear him laugh. Until now he'd been acting as if he were going to his doom, in spite of her telling him that everything would work out just fine. He undid the top buttons of his coat and fingered his shirt collar yet again.

'I keep feeling as if I'm going to choke.'

'Ma says the cloth will soften, given time.'

'By then I'll have stopped breathing.'

They laughed again.

Elfie wondered why men had to wear such uncomfortable clothes. Not Pa Bigsby, of course. He had more sense. He wore a soft white lawn shirt and a purple silk cravat with his lilac suit.

She leaned over the side rail, watching the people hurrying to work. Men mostly, some dressed like Joe in black suits, others even posher in frock coats and top hats. Then there were those who wore shabbier clothes and cloth caps. Women were out buying vegetables from the costermongers' barrows or pushing prams piled high with washing to the laundry. Kids trailed along to school, scuffing their feet on the pavement.

Elfie wished Pa Bigsby would let her go with Joe every morning but she knew there was no point in even asking. You had to be half dead and unable to get out of bed before he'd let you off school. He said education was the key to a good life. Look at Joe! He was held up as their example. He'd sat the School

Board's Matriculation examinations and come out with brilliant marks in English, Latin, Greek and History. That, Pa Bigsby said, had laid the foundations for him to embark on a successful career.

Joe was looking gloomy again. Ma had said he was bound to be nervous. Everyone was when they started something new. What about Elfie herself, the first day she'd come to the *Pig*? She'd tried to run away when she'd found they were going to strip off her old clothes and dump her in a tin basin before pouring paraffin over her head to get rid of the nits. She was glad now of course that she'd stayed. Who'd want beasts in their hair and clothes in tatters?

The bus wove its way down the length of St John Street, stopping at intervals for passengers to get on and off. One sudden jolt nearly sent them flying over the rail. A cart had cut out of a side street into the path of the bus. The horses reared and neighed and the drivers shouted at each other. For two or three minutes oaths flew backwards and forwards. A bus behind them was bleeping its horn.

'I hope they don't waste too much time.' Joe took out the fob watch Pa Bigsby had given him for his fourteenth birthday. 'Twenty to nine. I don't want to be late.'

'Not on your first morning.'

'Not on any morning!'

'You got twenty minutes still.'

'*You've got!*' said Joe.

'You're getting to be as bad as Pa Bigsby.'

That made him grin at least.

Elfie knew he would hate to be even a minute late. He always did things carefully, and on time, unlike her. She was inclined to wait until the last minute and rush in at top speed. Ma Bigsby said she could always relax when Elfie was out with Joe for she knew he'd keep her out of mischief. Or at least he would do his best.

In the end the cart gave way, the driver still cursing. The bus was a lot bigger and higher than his vehicle.

When they reached Smithfield Market, Joe rebuttoned his coat and checked that his collar was sitting straight.

'Soon be our stop.' He had done a trial run with Pa the day before. 'Got your brolly?'

Elfie fished it out from under the seat.

'Right then, let's go!'

Joe led the way, with both of them holding on to the rail going down. The bus had picked up speed and was swaying from side to side. The driver must be trying to make up for lost time.

'Holborn Circus,' called out the conductor, tugging the bell.

The bus lurched to a halt and they leapt out onto the pavement. Joe examined his watch again.

'Twelve minutes to go. Tomorrow I'll take an earlier bus.'

He set off at a brisk pace down Fetter Lane. Elfie had to run to keep up with his long stride. They cut through a side street and emerged into Chancery Lane.

This was where the lawyers had their offices. A lot

of them did, anyway. The brass plates gleamed in the dull light. It had started to drizzle but it didn't seem worth putting up their brollies when they were so near. Joe replaced his bowler hat and Elfie suppressed a giggle.

They crossed the road. They had arrived at their destination with a full five minutes to spare, which Elfie considered to be plenty. This was the first time she had been here. Her father had moved from his previous office in Covent Garden a couple of months back. He'd said it was more convenient, with the law courts being close by.

'I expect Papa will be in. He's always up with the lark. That's what his wife says.'

Elfie supposed that she should call Mrs Trelawney her stepmother but she couldn't quite think of her like that. She had a half-sister, too, Rosalind, who was seven years old. A spoiled brat, but Elfie could cope with her.

Joe was staring at the brass plate beside the door.

'What's up?' asked Elfie.

'Read it!'

She read aloud:

'Alfred Jonathan Trelawney

'Reginald Basildon-Blunt

'Solicitors-at-law,

'Reginald Basildon-Blunt,' repeated Elfie. 'Who the heck's he? What's his name doing there?'

'Your father must have taken on a partner.'

'You're going to be his partner.'

'Don't be silly!' Joe sounded a bit snappy, for him.

He was still staring at the plate. He must have a bad feeling about this. So did she, a bit. Her father had never mentioned this new man to her. But then why should he? It had nothing to do with her and she didn't usually come to his office. On Sundays she visited him at his house on Hampstead Heath.

'I expect Mr Basildon-Blunt will be nice, Joe. My father wouldn't take him on if he weren't.'

Joe stepped up, took hold of the brass knocker and banged it, not too hard. The stout mahogany door opened almost immediately and a thin man with a sharp face poked his head out. He was dressed totally in black, with only the white of his face to relieve it. He frowned.

'Yes?' he said. That was all. He couldn't take his eyes off Joe, who stood at Elfie's side.

'Joe's come to start work,' she informed him. 'I'm Elfie, Mr Trelawney's daughter.'

'Mr Trelawney is expecting me,' said Joe in a firm, clear voice.

'The man cleared his throat and coughed behind his hand. It was white and bony too. After another hesitation he said, 'You'd better come in.'

'I think we had,' agreed Elfie cheerfully. 'It's starting to rain and I've got my best cape on.'

The man held the door back and permitted them to enter.

'Are you Mr Basildon-Blunt?' asked Elfie.

'Oh no! My name is Parker.' Another cough behind his hand. 'Mr Trelawney is in his office with a client. He requested that you wait in the waiting room. Please come this way.'

They followed him along the corridor into the room. He held out his white hand but did not look directly at Joe's face while asking, 'May I take your coat?'

Joe undid his coat, his fingers fumbling with the buttons, and handed it to Mr Parker.

'And your hat?'

Joe surrendered that too. Elfie thought he would probably be glad if it were to get lost.

'And you, miss? Do you wish to take off your cloak?'

'I can throw it over a chair.'

'I'm afraid that would not do, miss. Not if a client were to arrive.'

Elfie gave up her cloak but she was annoyed. She hadn't liked the way the man had spoken to her. What was her father doing with a man like him in his office?

He left the room but before closing the door he took a quick glance back. Nosey Parker! Maybe he thought they were about to steal the brass fire tongs!

They moved in towards the coal fire that crackled and glowed in the grate. Elfie squatted down to warm her hands. She'd forgotten her gloves.

The door reopened and they looked round, expecting to see Elfie's father. But another man stood in the doorway. Just for a moment Elfie thought she recognised him but she couldn't think from where. He had a red face and a heavy jaw shaped like a spade and he was looking astounded at what he saw before him. His eyes travelled from Joe to Elfie and back again.

Elfie jumped up. 'You must be Mr Basildon-Blunt!'

'And who are you, miss?'

'I'm Mr Trelawney's daughter.'

'His daughter?' He frowned. Then a light seemed to dawn somewhere at the back of his mind.

'Oh, yes! The *other* one. He did happen to mention it. You live in some sort of pub in Stoke Newington, I believe?'

'I'm going to hate this man,' thought Elfie. 'I'm really going to hate him.'

'It's in Green Lanes,' she told him. 'Called the *Pig and Whistle*.'

'The *Pig and Whistle*?'

'It's a great place. Ma and Pa Bigsby run it.'

'Ma and Pa Bigsby?' The man laughed. It was not a jolly laugh. 'Sounds like a circus act.'

'Pa Bigsby's a brilliant scholar. Knows everything there is to know.'

'I very much doubt that!'

The man, though, could not keep his eyes off Joe, who was standing up to his full height. 'And you, boy? What do you think you are doing here? You have no right to be in this room!'

Without giving Joe a chance to reply he opened the door and yelled, 'Parker!'

Parker reappeared so quickly that Elfie realised he must have been eavesdropping from behind the door.

'Mr Basildon-Blunt?' he said, bowing his head.

'Parker, please take this person through to the back premises. I presume you have employed him as some kind of boot boy?'

'Not, he has not,' cried Elfie. 'He's going to be an office boy.'

'An *office* boy!' The man uttered a short derisive laugh. 'Not on your life! There is no way I am going to have a darkie working in my office.'

Joe flinched but said nothing.

'It's not nice to call someone that!' snapped Elfie. 'It's bad manners.'

'Who says?'

'Pa Bigsby.'

'Oh, my, the brilliant Mr Bigsby!'

'This is my father's office! He can have who he wants working here, so there!'

'It is *my* office too, girl. And please do not speak to me again in such a manner! I am your father's partner. And if I *were* your father – God forbid! – I would have you whipped for your insolence.'

Joe had remained quite still and silent throughout. His big black eyes looked sombre in his brown face. Soulful, Florrie would have called them. Joe could smile and laugh as much as anyone else but sometimes he had that other look. As Florrie said, it wasn't always easy for him. It was all right when he was in the

Pig where no one would dare insult him. If they did Pa would read the Riot Act and Ma would have them out on their ear on the pavement in a flash.

Elfie knew it would be difficult for Joe to say anything. She just could not understand how her father would take on such an unpleasant, horrible, rude man as this Mr Reginald Basildon-Blunt! Nor could she understand why he had not explained to his new partner that Joe was black.

They heard voices outside. One belonged to Elfie's father. He seemed to be saying goodbye to someone.

'Parker,' ordered Mr Basildon-Blunt, 'ask Mr Trelawney to come in here straightaway!'

Parker slid off at once and a moment later Elfie's father entered the room. She flew into his arms.

He hugged her tight, then released her to turn towards his partner. They faced each other.

'I would like an explanation, Alfred!'

'I presume you mean –?'

Basildon-Blunt cut him off. 'You know damned well what I mean! Why did you not tell me that this new office boy you had engaged was *black*?'

'I thought it better that you should meet Joe first and see what a fine young man he is. He is an excellent scholar. He gained high marks in the Matric in English, Latin and Greek –'

'I don't give a fig about marks! What about our clients?'

'What about them?' Elfie's father was keeping calm.

His partner was not. 'They would not care to do

business with a firm that employed negroes. They would object. Most strongly.'

'I have many enlightened clients who will not.'

'And I have many who will! Some might well leave.'

'Then let them!'

'*Let* them?' Basildon-Blunt's face had by now turned the same shade as their turkey-red carpet in the sitting room at the *Pig*. 'We are talking about *business*, Alfred. Money! We need clients to bring it in. We cannot exist on thin air.'

Maybe this would all turn out for the good, Elfie was thinking. Her father could get rid of the man and work on his own again with Joe to help him. She glanced at Joe. He was standing like a statue, staring ahead.

'Sometimes I think you do not live in the real world, Alfred,' said Basildon-Blunt, calming down a little. 'You know as well as I do how people feel, even if you will not admit it.'

'Things are changing, Reginald,' said Alfred Trelawney quietly. 'There are a number of students from the Empire studying law in London now .'

'Yes, Australia and New Zealand. Or Canada.'

'From India and the West Indies too. I have a good friend from Trinidad who is currently studying law at the Inns of Court.'

'Indeed?' Basildon-Blunt's eyes narrowed. They reminded Elfie of a ferret she'd seen once down at the docks. 'I did not know you kept such company. Perhaps you should watch your step, Alfred.'

He turned on his heel and strode from the room, letting the door slam behind him.

Elfie gasped. It had sounded as if he were threatening her father. He must not know that her father's own grandmother had come from Bermuda.

Joe spoke now. 'Mr Trelawney, maybe I should go.'

'You most certainly will not.'

'I don't want to cause trouble.'

'Joe, sometimes it is necessary to stand one's ground. This is one of them. You are an intelligent boy and I want you to work for me.'

'But Mr Basildon-Blunt?'

'Don't worry, I will deal with him.' Elfie's father turned to her. 'I think it is time you returned to the *Pig and Whistle*, love. I promised Mr Bigsby that you would not stay long. Come, I'll see you to the door.'

On her way out Elfie looked back. 'It'll be all right, Joe,' she said, though she didn't feel at all sure that it would.

Nosey Parker was lurking at the end of the corridor.

'He didn't used to work for you, did he, Papa?' she said in a low voice. 'Mr Parker?'

'No, he came with my new partner.' Her father's voice changed and became more brisk. 'Now, have you got your brolly, love? Good. You'll need to put it up. I don't want you arriving back soaked to get a row from Mrs Bigsby.' He embraced her and said he would collect her on Sunday as usual.

Elfie unfurled her umbrella, said goodbye to her

father and stepped out into the rain. On the pavement she paused to look round. Joe was standing at the window. His face was blurred behind the curtain of rain. She waved but he seemed not to see her. He seemed to be staring into space.

Chapter Three:
Trouble All the Way

Elfie hated umbrellas but she was glad Ma had made her take one today. She splashed her way back towards the bus stop thinking about Joe and her father's horrible new partner. Why had he taken him on? That was what she couldn't understand. He'd done all right on his own before. He'd said he liked it that way for then he could choose his own clients. It was a bit of a mystery to her, this one. She wondered what the brilliant detective Sherlock Holmes would make of it. Something was teasing at the corner of her mind. She still had a funny feeling that she'd seen Mr Reginald Basildon-Blunt before. But how could she have? She didn't go about lawyers' offices and she was sure he'd never been in the *Pig*. It was plain he'd never heard of it before she'd mentioned it.

'Spare a copper for the starvin', miss.'

The voice stopped Elfie dead. It had come from

a doorway. She peered in. A girl was curled up in the corner with a wad of newspaper around her shoulders. A piece of cardboard propped up in front her said:

'STARVIN

HOMLESS'

And in front of the notice sat a tin lid with a couple of farthings in it.

'Gertie!' gasped Elfie.

Gertie didn't recognise her, not the way she was now, dressed in a blue cloak with a fur-trimmed hood. It scarcely mattered that there was a slight smudge on the velvet. Later, Elfie was to wish that she'd walked straight on by.

'It's me – Elfie,' she said.

'My Gawd, Elfie, I'd never have knowed you, all toshed up in them clothes. Where did you nick 'em?'

'I didn't.'

Elfie furled her umbrella and stepped inside the shelter. Gertie pulled herself up into a sitting position. Her hair looked filthy and her dress was in rags. Once Elfie had looked like that herself.

'I've got a place to live now.'

'Ain't you the lucky one! Lord save us, you've turned into a right little lady.'

It was the first time anyone had said that to Elfie! Ma was always telling her she should be more lady-like now that she was twelve and to stop sliding down the banisters and vaulting over the staircase.

'Where you dossin' then?' asked Gertie.

'A pub.'

'Pub? Give you gin, do they?'

'They do not!' Ma would have a fit at the very idea.

'But they make you sing for your supper, I bet? Scrub floors and all that?'

'We have to do some chores but we get lessons, too, from the owner, Pa Bigsby. I've learned to read. And write.'

'Cor blimey, sounds like you landed on your feet, Elf. Funny kind of pub though giving lessons.'

'Pa Bigsby and his wife take in orphans, you see, and give them a home and an education.'

'Would they have room for another?'

'I don't think so.' Elfie felt awkward now.

'I wouldn't be good enough, is that it?'

'No, it's just that there are eleven of us already and normally they only take ten.'

'How'd you git in then? Flash your big brown eyes at them? Where is this place? What's it called?'

'The *Pig and Whistle*. It's in Stoke Newington.' Elfie bit her lip but there was no taking it back now.

'I 'spect you could talk them into takin' jest one more,' said Gertie in a wheedling voice that Elfie remembered. Gertie had always been good when it came to begging. She'd put a hand on a man's arm and look up into his face. She'd tell him what a nice gentleman he was and he'd usually give her a penny or two and by the time he'd walked off she'd have filched something else out of his coat pocket with her free hand.

'I'll ask.' Elfie was anxious now to get away. She'd

never liked Gertie. In fact, she'd hated her. Gertie had tried to steal things from her bag more than once when she was asleep and one night they'd had a bad fight. Gertie had ended up with a black eye and Elfie with a long scratch down her cheek that had taken more than a week to heal. Most of the kids who slept rough under the arches fought and stole from each other.

'You do that. You ask.' Gertie smirked, knowing that Elfie would not. 'How's about letting me have that fine cloak you're wearin'? You could always git another.'

'No!' Elfie held it tightly round her. Gertie would not expect her to give it up. She'd think her daft if she did. She was just trying to goad her.

'Mean, ain't yer? But you must have you somethin' in your pocket you can give us?'

'I've some money for my bus.'

'Oh my, go on the bus, do we? No walkin' for little ladies in them fancy leather boots! In that case you can let me have your brolly to keep meself dry. You're not needin' it, are you, not with that fancy bit of fur on yer head?' Gertie put her hand round Elfie's ankle and held it fast, grinning up at her.

Elfie knew she could soon push Gertie away if she had to. She could wallop her too if she were to turn nasty. But Gertie probably was half starving and she had no coat to cover herself. And it was raining. Elfie decided she'd give her the umbrella and keep back a penny so that she could take one bus at least. She dug into her pocket and brought up some coins.

'Here!' She dropped three into the tin lid. 'You can have the umbrella too.'

'Ta very much. What a nice girl you is. Ever so kind.'

Elfie jerked her ankle free.

'You've something left there in yer paw.' Gertie pointed at Elfie's hand.

'One penny, that's all.'

'All? It'd buy me a cup o' tea and a sugar bun.'

'I've given you thruppence.'

'But it'd be even kinder of you if you was to give me the other penny an' all.'

'I need it for the bus,' said Elfie firmly, putting it back in her pocket.

'Scum!' cried Gertie and summoning up her energy she spat. Elfie stepped back, but the blob of spittle landed on the front of her boot.

For a moment Elfie did almost kick out; she was sorely tempted. Then she thought of Pa Bigsby. She backed out of the doorway and walked quickly away before she could change her mind. Gertie's mocking laughter rang in her ears.

The rain was not letting up. Everything was against her. She trudged on, through the puddles, head down, water dripping from her hood onto her face. All the people she passed seemed to be carrying big black umbrellas. At least Gertie's spit had been washed off her boot. She *hated* Gertie! Really hated her. She wished she had kicked her good and hard. *No, you don't!* She could hear Pa Bigsby's voice in her head.

He'd tell her to remember that Gertie was homeless, a poor orphan on the streets, just as she herself had been. She should feel charitable towards her. She should feel pity for her. She did, but she still hated her. At the moment she wasn't too fond of herself either. Perhaps she should have given up the extra penny. It would have done more for Gertie than for her. She knew too well what Gertie's life would be like. She almost turned back but Gertie would only mock her. Elfie felt all mixed up in her head, what with her father's new partner being rude to Joe, and then coming across someone from her old life. It was not turning out to be a very good day after all.

And by the time she made it back to the *Pig* she'd be soaked to the skin. Her red velvet dress might be ruined. She'd get a row from Ma about that and another from Pa for being late.

She wasn't even sure where she was now! This wasn't the route they had come by. A pale green bus had stopped at the traffic lights. She peered through the rain. It was going to King's Cross. That would take her at least part of the way. She raced towards the next stop and arrived just as the bus was pulling in. She paid her penny and went inside to recover her breath. It would still be a long way up to Stoke Newington from King's Cross but her luck might turn and she'd get a lift with a carter. They were coming and going to the station all the time.

But this morning they were not. When she left the

bus there was no sign of a cart at all. The rain couldn't be keeping all the carters indoors! They had to earn their living. She found some shelter under an overhang and darted out from time to time to take a look. One or two carts did rumble by but they were going in the wrong direction. Finally she saw one coming out of the station that she recognised. The carter was Billy's friend, Tommy. She ran towards him waving and he brought his horse to a halt.

Yes, he was going up Green Lanes and she could have a lift but she'd have to sit on top of the wood. He had a full load.

'You in your good clothes . . .' He looked doubtful.

'They're not good now. They're soaking.'

'Right you are then! Up you get!'

She climbed up and they cantered off. Elfie had ridden on the back of his cart before so she knew to cling on tightly for the corners.

Just as they reached the *Pig and Whistle* the rain stopped.

Elfie jumped down. 'Thanks, Tommy.'

'Any time, luv.'

Sad Sid, one of their regulars, was leaning against the pub wall, waiting for it to open. He was holding a broken old umbrella over his head. Most of the spikes were bent. He looked a sorry sight.

'Where you bin, Elfie? Why are you not at your lessons?'

'I was seeing Joe to his work.'

'Ain't he the lucky fellow?' said Sad Sid in his mournful voice.

Elfie hoped so.

She went inside. There was no sign of anyone downstairs. The old pram was missing from the scullery so Ma must have taken Cuddles and gone shopping. Cuddles was three years old now but they never called him by his real name – Caspar – it didn't seem to suit him.

Elfie decided she'd wait to change into dry clothes. She reckoned that if Pa saw how wet she was he'd feel sorry for her and not give her a lecture. Well, that was what she hoped. She dashed up the stairs to the schoolroom and flung open the door.

Standing in front of the class beside Pa Bigsby was a man with a wispy goatee beard, wearing a greenish-black frock-coat and spotted spats.

'Oh no!' she cried, though she did it inside her head, which was just as well. If she'd spoken aloud she'd have been in even more trouble.

Mr Ramsbottom was an inspector from the Schools Board, come to check up on their progress. When he'd visited them last year Elfie had made such a mess of everything she'd almost got the school failed. He'd asked her to recite a poem and hadn't been at all pleased when she'd rattled off *Roses are red, violets are blue, sugar is sweet and so are you.* He'd been looking for something more scholarly, he'd said. Joe had saved the day by reciting the whole of 'Drake's Drum' in his rich deep voice. But Joe, their top scholar, wasn't here to save them today.

'Elfie, child, where have you been?' Pa Bigsby looked at her aghast. 'You're soaking wet. Did you not have an umbrella?'

'I did but I sort of lost it.'

'Go at once and change into some dry clothes and come back and join us. Mr Ramsbottom has just arrived.'

That was bad luck. It was following her everywhere she went. Even the rain had waited to stop until she'd arrived home.

'And do not delay!' added Pa Bigsby. He knew Elfie too well.

As she closed the door she heard the inspector say, 'I remember that girl.'

She stripped off the wet clothes and put on some dry ones. Then, with a sigh, she returned to the schoolroom and took her seat.

Mr Ramsbottom was touring around the desks inspecting everyone's writing books. He reached Elfie. She smelt him coming. The stench from his frock-coat was enough to make you gag when he leant over. And he had the same filthy fingernails as before.

'I seem to recall that your calligraphy was very poor last year,' he said.

'Elfie had not long joined us,' put in Pa Bigsby. 'And had not had the benefit of education until then. I think you will find her hand much improved.'

Elfie's writing was still not her best point. Pa always

told her to take more time for that way she'd manage to keep between the lines better. She was too impatient.

Mr Ramsbottom humphed and scrabbled in his raggy beard. Elfie was convinced he had nits in it.

'It's a bit better,' he conceded, 'but there is still room for considerable improvement.'

She made a face behind his back as he moved on to Billy, whose writing did not please him too much either. Ivy's did. He commended her and she turned round to stick out her tongue at Elfie. Elfie could not be bothered doing it back.

He examined their sum jotters and was unable to find much fault, then they laboured through a list of questions he had drawn up on geography and history. Finally, it was time for Recitation.

'I think we shall start with you, miss.' He stabbed his finger at Elfie. 'And none of your roses are red this time!' He seemed to think he had made a joke.

She was ready for him. 'The Daffodil,' she announced, 'by William Wordsworth.'

'Proceed!'

'*I wander'd lonely as a cloud*
That floats on high o'er vales and hills,
When all at once I saw a crowd,
A host of golden daffodils . . .'

Elfie longed to see a host of golden daffodils. There would be a few in the park at the top of the road come March but not "a host". She said every line of the poem perfectly smoothly, not stumbling over a single word. When she'd finished Mr Ramsbottom was silent for a moment.

'Do you know where that poem is set?' he asked. Perhaps he hoped to catch her out.

'The Lake District.'

'I intend to take the children there in springtime,' said Pa Bigsby. 'To see the daffodils.'

There was a buzz of excitement in the class.

'Quiet now, children.' Pa turned to the inspector. 'Mr Ramsbottom, I aim to give the children in my care a well-rounded comprehensive education in the arts, sciences and humanities. Physical well-being is not neglected either. Regular exercise is taken in the park and in summer I employ a cricket coach. I believe the game of cricket to be highly valuable. Even our girls show aptitude though our star player is Joe. He is an excellent overarm bowler. You remember Joe, who recited "Drake's Drum" so well?'

'You mean the black one?'

Pa Bigsby ignored that. 'He is currently employed by a legal firm in Chancery Lane.'

That was one in the eye for Old Scabbybottom, thought Elfie.

'Is there anything else you wish to see, or to ask, Mr Ramsbottom?' said Pa. 'No? In that case, please stand, everybody, and say good morning to Mr Ramsbottom.'

'Good morning, Mr Ramsbottom,' they chanted.

'Good morning,' he mumbled in return and Pa Bigsby guided him out of the room. Elfie thought the inspector had been miffed that he hadn't found more to criticise. When Pa returned he complimented them all on their performance. Even the little ones had done exceedingly well with their letters and numbers.

'And now, Elfie,' said Pa, 'you must tell us how Joe got on.'

Chapter Four:
Saturday, Secrets
and Suppers

Pa Bigsby received a letter from Elfie's father by the Friday morning post.

My dear Mr Bigsby,

As you may know, we close the office at midday on Saturday. I thought that I would like to give Joe a small treat to mark the end of his first week's work. I am extremely pleased with him. He learns fast and is proving to be a great help to me. I should like to take him and Elfie to a restaurant for lunch and, since it happens to be my birthday, it would be a treat for me too!

I trust this would not inconvenience you in any way and look forward to your reply.

With kindest regards,
Alfred Trelawney

'I didn't know it was his birthday,' cried Elfie. 'I'll have to buy him a present.' She only had tuppence left from her pocket money but she should be able to buy something. 'I can go, can't I?'

'You would have to attempt not to mislay another umbrella though.'

'Oh, I wouldn't, Pa!'

Her going-out clothes were fit to be worn again. Ma, after giving her a lecture about umbrellas costing money, had dried her red dress on the pulley and steam-ironed the velvet so that it looked fit to wear again. Her cloak, too. Her father often wanted to buy her more clothes but Ma wouldn't allow her to have too many at the *Pig*. She said it was unfair to the other children.

'Can I, Pa?'

'Yes, of course you may go, Elfie. Especially since it is your father's birthday. But there is one thing that you must promise me, apart from not losing an umbrella.'

'I'll come straight home this time, honest!'

'I am assuming you will. Besides, Joe will see that you do. No, I want you to promise that you will not boast to Ivy about going to a restaurant.'

He raised his hand as Elfie was about to protest. She had been going to say that she wouldn't dream of doing that, though, if she were to be cross-your-heart honest, she knew she might just have let it slip.

'You must understand that she does not get the treats that you do,' Pa went on. 'Simply tell her and the others that you are going to meet your father in town.'

Elfie promised.

'Joe does seem to be doing exceedingly well,' observed Pa Bigsby as he refolded the letter. 'I am not surprised. He seems happy there?'

'He'd be even happier if it weren't for that nasty old Blunt-Face.'

'Elfie, you must not talk like that!' Pa wasn't really annoyed though. He had heard all about Mr Reginald Basildon-Blunt and agreed that he did not sound an agreeable man. Not one with whom he himself would wish to strike up an acquaintance.

'He's 'orrible – sorry, Pa, horrible – to Joe. Joe says he never passes up the chance to snub him.'

'I am aware of that. But I think Joe can cope with it. I have had a long talk with him. You see, Elfie, until now Joe has lived in our safe little circle here at the *Pig*. We know him and love him. He is one of us. And the customers have known him since he was a small child. But it is right that he should go out into the world now even though it might be hard for him. You can understand that?'

Elfie nodded.

'It seems that he has little to do with this other lawyer, which is fortunate. He appears to work only with your father. And he, Elfie, is an admirable man. A man of principle. Not many lawyers in the city would be willing to give a black boy such a chance.'

Joe's handwriting was excellent so he had been given documents to copy and envelopes to address. He also went out twice a day to visit the post office and deliver statements to offices round about. That was the part of the job Elfie would have fancied. The only part. Sitting on a high stool at a desk concentrating on making the loops of your letters perfect did not appeal to her, any more than sewing buttons on shirts at the factory had. She'd only lasted a day when Ma had sent her there with Mabel and Ivy. They were now employed a few hours a day by a Miss Swanston to sew lace around the edges of pillow cases. Mabel liked the work. Ivy grumbled. But Miss Swanston was kind and gave them lumps of Turkish Delight, which didn't bother Elfie since she hated its gooey sweetness. Her afternoon work was doing delivery runs with Billy for local businesses. Sometimes the stuff was heavy to hump about but her arms were strong, even if they were a bit on the skinny side, as Ma kept telling her. She was always saying that Elfie needed more beef on her bones.

'I shall now write a reply, Elfie,' said Pa, 'and you may convey it straightaway to the Post Office so that it will arrive in Chancery Lane by the late afternoon post.'

Pa Bigsby penned a brief note, wrote his signature with a flourish, slid the sheet of paper into an envelope and stamped his seal on the back in red wax.

'There!' He presented it to Elfie. He also reached into his pocket and took out a sixpence. 'Buy your father a present for his birthday. And don't dilly-dally on the way! I shall shortly be teaching a lesson on the Wars of the Roses.'

That sounded interesting so Elfie put a spurt on. She ran all the way to the post office and dispatched the letter.

'It'll get there by teatime, won't it?' she asked anxiously.

'It will,' said the man behind the counter, looking at the address. 'Chancery Lane. Guaranteed.'

As Elfie turned to leave, Mr Ramsbottom, the school inspector, entered. There was no chance of sliding past him.

'Should you not be at your lessons, girl? You surely know you are obliged to attend school full-time until you are twelve years old. What age are you now?'

'Twelve.'

Next year she could stop her lessons if she wanted to, though not really, for Pa Bigsby would never let her. She didn't want to, either. She enjoyed most of them. It was just things like algebra and trigonometry that got her down.

'I understood from Mr Bigsby that the entire morning was spent on school work?'

'I had to post a letter for him.'

'That could have been done in the afternoon.'

'It was an emergency. Matter of life and death.'

The inspector humphed and she dodged around him and made her escape.

She nipped into Mrs O'Grady's, the confectioner's. After giving it some consideration she decided on a large box of violet chocolates. They were Ma's favourites. She always said you couldn't beat them, they were a real treat.

'They're for my father's birthday,' she told Mrs O'Grady.

'Mr Bigsby?'

'No, I've got a real father.'

'That's nice for you, dear.'

'But Pa Bigsby's like a father too.'

'I'm sure he is. He's a grand man so he is.'

Mrs O'Grady hailed from Ireland, which you'd know from the way she talked. Like Ma Bigsby and Dowdy. There seemed to be a lot of Irish people around these parts. Ma said they came because Ireland was a poor country and in London there was work to be found, if you were lucky.

'Would you like me to put a ribbon round the box for you?' asked Mrs O'Grady.

'Yes, please!'

Mrs O'Grady put an extra chocolate in the box and then tied it up with a length of red satin ribbon, finishing off with a bow.

'I'm sure he'll be dead happy with that,' she declared.

Elfie thought so too. She thanked Mrs O'Grady and left the shop feeling pleased with her purchase. Her smile disappeared when she saw the school inspector coming out of the post office. She took to her heels.

꧁⊙⊙꧂

The restaurant was in the Strand. The tablecloths were of fresh white linen, the cutlery real silver, the tumblers cut-glass and the straight-backed waiters looked like lawyers in their black suits and white shirts. Elfie was amazed at how easily they carried their silver trays aloft on one white-gloved hand. Her father had taken her out for a meal before but only to a chop house.

'Miss,' said their waiter in a snooty voice, as he unrolled her napkin and waited for her to sit back so that he could spread it over her knee.

He then unwrapped the napkin for her father, who tucked it into his collar, like a bib, the way Pa Bigsby wore his. The waiter moved on, ignoring Joe.

'I shall not be giving him much of a gratuity,' said Alfred Trelawney. 'Possibly nothing.'

'It doesn't matter,' said Joe, unwrapping his own serviette.

When the waiter returned to take their order again he did not look at Joe.

'Would you please give my friend here some water?' asked Alfred Trelawney, indicating Joe.

For a moment Elfie thought the man was not going to oblige. When he did, he averted his eyes and managed to spill some water which ran down the table onto Joe's lap. Elfie felt like throwing the rest of the water in the jug over the waiter but restrained herself. Her father would not be pleased if she did, and it was his birthday. She confined herself to giving the man a nasty look.

'I shall have a word with the manager.' Alfred Trelawney rose from his seat.

'You don't have to,' said Joe, his brow furrowed.

'Yes, I do, Joe.'

They watched him approach the manager and engage him in conversation. They saw the manager shrug and indicate some of the other people in the room.

'He would rather I was not here,' said Joe quietly. 'A lot of them would.'

He had been subjected to a number of stares as they came in. They had been given a table in the corner of the restaurant behind a potted plant with large spreading leaves.

'The manager apologises,' said Alfred Trelawney, when he returned to the table. 'Now then, we are going to enjoy our lunch!'

'That was a fib about the manager,' thought Elfie. Everybody told them at times, even Ma Bigsby. When she wanted you to do something unpleasant or eat some kind of food you didn't like, such as fish roe, she'd say, 'Eat up now, it's good for the brain.' Not Pa, though. You could always count on him to tell the truth. Like Joe.

Elfie gave her father his birthday present and he declared himself absolutely delighted with the violet chocolates.

'My favourites,' he said. Elfie suspected he was telling another fib.

They had brown Windsor soup, followed by roast beef and Yorkshire pudding and jam roly-poly to finish. By the end of the meal Elfie could scarcely move. Her father decided they should take a stroll along the Strand.

'A little fresh air and exercise will do us good.'

Being Saturday afternoon, the city was quiet. After they had walked for a short while Elfie's father examined his pocket watch and said he was sorry but they must turn back now. Mrs Trelawney had organised an evening party for his birthday.

'Two parties in one day! Am I not fortunate?'

He had parked his motor car near the restaurant. Made by a firm in France called Renault, the vehicle was long and black and shiny, with an open top. Both Elfie and Joe found it amazing. Since there was only one passenger seat Elfie had to sit on Joe's knee. Her father gave her a leather helmet to wear, similar to his own. It was too large and came right down over her eyebrows so that she could scarcely see out, but he insisted she wear it, lest she got a chill. To Joe he lent a thick woollen scarf to wind around his head.

'I have to stop in Islington for a few minutes,' he told them. 'To pick up something for my wife from her dressmaker.'

They zoomed through the streets at a steady twenty miles an hour. People turned their heads as they passed by.

Alfred Trelawney parked in a side street in the centre of Islington.

'Won't be long,' he said as he jumped out and made for a house across the road.

'He's so nice, your father,' said Joe. 'But do you know what I don't understand?'

'What?' asked Elfie.

'Why someone like him would take on Mr Basildon-Blunt as a partner. For he's not nice at all! There is something odd about that.' Joe's brow had that furrowed look again. It came on when he was troubled.

'What kind of odd?'

'I don't know exactly. He was so rude to your father yesterday. He came into his office shouting his head off.'

'Never! What was it about?'

'A client hadn't paid a bill.'

'So what did he say, old Blunt-Face?'

'I can remember his exact words, I was so startled. "You shouldn't have taken him on, Trelawney. You're a fool! You might have known he wouldn't pay. An ironmonger! We shouldn't have anything to do with trade. We won't in future. Nor do we wish to have anything to do with injury claims at the docks." That was how he spoke to your father, as if he had the right to dictate to him.'

'How dare he!' Elfie clenched her fists. 'I wish I'd have been there. I'd have given him what for! So what did my father say?'

'Not much. Just that the ironmonger had needed help. He was embarrassed. Old Blunt-Face then said, "This is not to happen again, Trelawney!" and left. Your father just sat there staring at the wall.'

'That's terrible!'

'It's almost as if Blunt-Face has got some hold over your father.'

'Here – he's coming now,' said Elfie quickly.

Elfie's father was carrying a parcel. He asked Elfie if she could manage to hold it on her knee. 'Without crumpling it?' he added anxiously.

'Is it a new dress for Mrs Trelawney?'

'It is, to wear tonight.'

'What colour is it?'

'Old rose, I believe the shade is called.'

'I expect she'll look lovely in it.'

'I expect she will.' His voice seemed flat. It did not sound like the voice of someone who was looking forward to his own birthday party.

He laid it carefully on her knee and she put both hands on top so that it would not blow off. Her father said he would reduce the speed to cut down the wind. The parcel survived the journey to the *Pig and Whistle* intact. Elfie was glad to pass it over and take her helmet off. She shook her head free.

She was still fizzing inside about that horrible old Blunt-Face being so rude to her father. She hadn't been able to enjoy the ride for thinking about it.

Billy came running out of the pub door. He must have heard the car.

'I'll give you a spin tomorrow, Billy,' Alfred Trelawney promised, 'when I come to collect Elfie.'

'Thanks, Mr Trelawney.'

Elfie's father gave her a hug and took off again.

'We've got a new girl in the house,' said Billy.

'How do you mean?' Elfie frowned. 'What new girl?'

'Friend of yours. Said she was. Said you told her to come to the *Pig*.'

'*Where is she?*'

'In the kitchen.'

Elfie pushed Billy aside and raced indoors.

Sitting at the end of the kitchen table digging into a plate of mutton stew was Gertie!

Chapter Five:
The Twelfth Orphan

Gertie lifted her head and grinned. Half of her front teeth were missing. Elfie remembered when she'd lost them in a fight with a boy called Froggy, who'd later been drowned in the Thames. Elfie wouldn't have been surprised if Gertie hadn't pushed him in.

'Wotcha, Elf! You was right. This is a good berth. Glad you didn't keep it to yerself. Never et such good mutton in me life.'

Gertie was wearing a blue flannel smock and black stockings and her face and hair looked *clean*. Elfie was speechless. Gertie's nickname in the gang had been Dirty Gertie but there was nothing dirty about her now. She must have had the whole treatment from Ma, been stood in the tin bath, had paraffin poured over her head to get rid of the nits and then shampooed with evil-smelling stuff and her body scrubbed down with carbolic soap. That was what had happened to Elfie herself when she'd first arrived. But then she'd been invited to *stay* at the *Pig*.

When Joe appeared in the doorway, Elfie saw Gertie's eyes flicker.

'Remember Joe? Remember that night when Froggy and his gang jumped on us near King's Cross? Joe had to go to the hospital. You can still see the scar on his cheek.'

'I weren't there.'

'Yes, you were!'

'No, I weren't.'

'Joe,' Elfie appealed to him, 'you remember seeing Gertie, don't you?'

'It was dark.' He shook his head. 'I didn't see all their faces. There were so many of them. I only remember his. Froggy's.'

'There you is!' crowed Gertie and she slurped down another spoonful of stew.

'She was there, Joe, I'm telling you!'

'Look, Elfie, let's leave it. It's over now.' Joe had never liked to talk about the incident. 'I must go and get changed.' He ran a finger inside his collar. When he came back from work he couldn't wait to to get out of his office clothes.

After he'd gone Elfie turned back to Gertie. 'You ain't staying.'

'Sez who?' Gertie gave her another grin.

'Sez me!'

'We'll have to see, won't we?'

Elfie ran from the room.

'Ma?' she yelled.

'She's in the bar,' said Mabel, who was coming down the stairs leading Cuddles by the hand.

Elfie found Ma polishing the brasses. She liked them to shine extra-brightly on a Saturday night.

'Ma,' gulped Elfie, 'that girl there in the kitchen –'

'Gertie?'

'You can't let her stay.'

'But you were the one that said for her to come here. You told her it was open door at the *Pig* and all orphans were welcome.'

'I never did! She's lying!'

'So how did she know where to find us?'

'I saw her in the street one day and she asked me where I was staying.' What a mistake that was, telling Gertie anything! Elfie couldn't believe she'd been so stupid. 'You can't let her stay, Ma. You can't! She steals.'

'I seem to remember you sometimes nicked the odd thing yourself afore you come here?'

Elfie felt her face heat up. Well, maybe she had, just the odd apple or a banana. 'Only when I was hungry.'

'Well, Gertie was hungry when she arrived on the step. Starvin', she said, hadn't eaten for a couple of days. She was shiverin' with the cold, too, poor child, and cryin' her eyes out.'

'She'd be putting it on. I know her!'

'Not very charitable of you, is it, Elfie?' said Pa, entering the bar. 'We took you in, didn't we?'

'I know, Pa. And I was real grateful. But she was in the gang that jumped on Joe and me last year. When Joe got his face cut.'

'We can't hold her responsible for what someone else did.'

'She was laughing her head off when it was going on.'

'I believe you knew those people yourself at one time?'

'I didn't go out with them when they were looking for trouble. I just slept under the bridges beside them. Pa, you can't trust Gertie, I'm telling you, you can't! She'll lie to you till she's blue in the face.'

'How did we know we could trust you in the beginning? We took the risk and are pleased that we did. On the whole,' Pa added with a smile.

'But you said you weren't going to take in any more orphans. There ain't – sorry, isn't – enough room.' Elfie was beginning to feel desperate. Surely they were not really and truly going to keep Gertie!

'She was limpin' and all,' put in Ma. 'She'd hurt her knee. I didn't have it in my heart to turn her away. She begged me to take her in. Poor starving girl.'

'I think it would be difficult for us to put her out on the street now, Elfie,' added Pa. 'Even you must see that?'

Elfie couldn't see it at all.

'You girls will just have to squash up in the bedroom,' said Ma. 'Or that alcove off the passage might take a mattress.'

'I hate her,' muttered Elfie as she turned away.

'Now, now!' Pa shook his head.

'If she stays I'm going! It's her or me.'

'You're just being silly, Elfie,' chided Ma, giving the brass candlestick in her hand a vigorous rub.

'I can go to my father's any time I want. He's said so.'

'We know that,' said Pa. 'And of course it is up to you. But we would all miss you if you went.'

'We would,' agreed Ma. 'Even if you do drive me to distraction at times.'

'People can change their ways, Elfie,' said Pa quietly. 'If they are given the chance of a decent life. Ma and I have found that over many years.'

Elfie had no answer to that. She left them and went barging into the hall to bump into Gertie herself.

'You were listening, weren't you?' demanded Elfie.

Gertie had that smirk on her face again. 'Why don't you jest go to your pa's? There'd be more room for me. You tellt me they were only wantin' to have eleven orphans anyway.'

Elfie caught Gertie by the hair and she screamed.

Out of the bar came Pa. Elfie let go of Gertie's hair.

'What's going on?'

'She were tryin' to yank me hair out o' the roots!' cried Gertie, clamping her hands to her head. 'Look, she's got a bit in her hand!'

Pa looked down at Elfie's hand.

'Only a wee bit. No more than a strand.' Elfie showed it reluctantly. 'She was snooping, Pa! Eavesdropping at the back of the door. I told you you couldn't trust her.'

'It is not permissible to pull hair out of another person's head.' Pa's voice was severe. 'You will please apologise to Gertie, Elfie.'

Apologise? To *Gertie*? He must be joking! She'd never apologise to Gertie for anything. Not for all the tea in China. She kept her mouth tight shut.

'Do as I say, Elfie, or else you will not be allowed to join us this evening.'

Elfie gulped.

'I'm waiting,' said Pa.

Elfie listened to the big hands on the kitchen clock ticking.

'Well? What is it to be? I can't wait here all day.'

'Sorry,' muttered Elfie, keeping her eyes on the floor.

Pa did not appear to be totally pleased but he returned to the bar and closed the door.

The grin on Gertie's face stretched from side to side like a slit melon. Then she broke into a cackle of laughter.

'You better watch yerself, Elf, or ye'll have to go to yer pa's whether you wants it or not.'

Gertie was tempting her, Elfie knew. She half raised her hand, then let it drop. She'd have loved to have given Gertie a right good wallop but to be banned on a Saturday night would be too big a price to pay.

This was the one night of the week that the older children were allowed in the bar. Well, almost in. They had to crouch in the doorway at first, though, gradually, with Ma being too busy to notice, they managed to inch their way a bit further into the room. It was the one night, too, that Pa made an entrance into the bar. Ma and Florrie served while he chatted to the customers and made sure that none took too much to drink. If they did they were asked to leave, unlike some of the public houses up the street.

Elfie loved Saturday nights, with the fire roaring up the chimney and the brasses gleaming in the gaslight. The bar was busy from the moment it opened. Joe, now that he was fourteen, was allowed to fetch and carry though not to serve. Elfie wished Ma would let her help but she said no, she was too young.

It was the one time in the week, too, that the men brought their wives. The ladies came decked out in their finery, looking quite different from when Elfie met them in the street wearing their aprons with their hair rolled up in rags. There was always lots of banter followed by gales of laughter. Sad Sid's friend Frankie played popular tunes on the harmonium and the customers called out requests for songs like 'Nellie Dean' and 'Knees up, Mother Brown'. Then the singing would start, led usually by Ma herself. She loved Irish songs. As Pa once said, she sang them from the heart.

This Saturday night, however, was different, for squatting beside Elfie was a girl whom she hated. Really hated. She couldn't help it even if Pa did think it wicked to hate another person. He might hate Gertie himself if she were to try to scratch his eyes out or if he'd seen her egging the gang on to kill Joe. She was sitting there grinning, trying to look as innocent as an angel.

Pa cast his eyes over them as he went by. 'All right, Gertie?'

'Yes, thank you, sir,' simpered Gertie.

He raised an eyebrow at Elfie, who was aware that she was probably scowling.

Then Frankie struck up 'Cockles and Mussels' and Ma broke into song

'*In Dublin's fair city, where the girls are so pretty . . .*'

The customers joined in. Mad Meg, Sad Sid's sister, was especially fond of the song so after Ma had finished she sang an extra verse all by herself, off-key as usual, but when she finished everyone applauded. She was known as Mad Meg, though, in Elfie's opinion, she wasn't that mad. She just liked to sing at the top of her voice and out of tune, sometimes on the street corner, and she waved to people going by in the buses. They usually waved back. So what was wrong with that? And she was good at needlework. She earned a few shillings a week embroidering pillow cases for a shop in the High Street. That helped feed herself and Sid. He was supposed to make boxes at home for a warehouse but he never seemed to finish many.

'She ain't arf a turn, that one,' said Gertie.

'Shut your mouth,' said Elfie.

She scrambled to her feet and edged nearer to the bar where she could watch Florrie serving. Florrie moved quickly up and down as she talked and laughed with the customers, and all the time her earrings swirled and birled and her pink satin blouse shone under the lights. She was wearing her three-tiered pearl choker and on the fourth finger of her left hand, her real gold engagement ring set with a moonstone. Dowdy hadn't been able to afford a diamond but Florrie didn't mind.

Elfie glanced around and Gertie caught her eye and raised her thumb.

'Got yourself a new pal, have you?' asked Sad Sid, who was standing at the bar.

Luckily Ma started on another favourite, 'The Rose of Tralee'.

'The pale moon was rising above the green mountains,
The sun was declining beneath the blue sea . . .'
The song drowned out Elfie's reply.

❧❦❧

Elfie opted to sleep in the alcove on the landing that night.

'That's not fair,' yowled Ivy. 'Why should you get to sleep there?'

'I put my mattress out first.'

'But it was your fault she come here.'

'Came.'

It was of some consolation to Elfie that Ivy didn't like Gertie either. For once they were in agreement. Grumbling, Ivy went off to join the others in the bedroom.

The alcove was rather narrow but Elfie found she

liked it out on the landing all by herself with no one snoring or coughing on either side of her. She heard Ma and Pa going to bed and their door closing. Ma was always tired after a long Saturday. They all were. The house creaked as if it too was settling down for the night. Elfie lay awake for a little while wondering how she could get rid of Gertie. Ivy had been right: it was her fault that Gertie had come to the *Pig*. So it was up to her to do something about it. But what? Neither Ma nor Pa would listen to her. Elfie yawned, and a moment later was asleep.

Outside, on the sign above the door, which swayed a little in the wind, the pig continued to keep guard and play his whistle.

Chapter Six:
Sunday in Hampstead

Gertie was already in the kitchen helping Ma prepare breakfast when Elfie went downstairs. She gave Elfie a triumphant little smile.

'Don't just stand there, Elfie,' said Ma Bigsby. 'Get the table set!'

After she'd done it Elfie went into the yard to get a breath of fresh air and count to ten. Ma said that was what you should do when you thought you might explode. Joe and Billy were out there rolling barrels, lining them up ready to be lifted by the drayman next morning.

'I could kill that Gertie!' said Elfie.

'Maybe you could.' Joe smiled. 'But I don't suppose you will.'

'How do you know?'

'You is in a snappy mood,' said Billy.

'Are,' said Elfie and went back inside. Everyone

was annoying her this morning. She was glad she was going to spend the day in Hampstead with her father. Though, on the other hand, when she came to think about it, she didn't like the idea of Gertie being here at the *Pig* when she herself would not be.

Before her father came to collect her they would go to church. Ma Bigsby went to the chapel with Dora and Nancy, who, like her, were Roman Catholics, while Pa took the rest of them around churches of every other denomination in London in turn. To widen their horizons, he said. Last week they had been to one called New Jerusalem in Islington for the first time. Today it was the Salvation Army, everyone's favourite. They loved the brass band and the chance to sing along. Better than sitting on a hard bench listening to a man drone on for hours, as far as Elfie was concerned. One of the men in the band was teaching Billy to play the bassoon.

The outing cheered Elfie. She walked back between Joe and Billy, ahead of Gertie, who was hanging on to Mabel's arm and looking up into her face.

'She's sucking up to Mabel.' Elfie groaned. 'It'd make you puke.'

'You can't let her go on bothering you,' said Joe, annoying Elfie again.

'What about you and old Blunt-Face? He bothers you, doesn't he?'

'I'm trying not to let him.'

Joe's face had taken on that closed-in look he

sometimes wore and Elfie had another reason to feel annoyed. This time it was with herself for bringing up the man's name. As Pa often told her, there were times when she should think before she spoke.

'Sorry,' she muttered.

'It's all right.'

Elfie's father was waiting outside the *Pig and Whistle*. The children broke into a run when they saw the motor car and Albert and Sam tried to climb into the passenger seat. Pa Bigsby called them back.

'It's all right,' said Alfred Trelawney. 'I'll give them a short spin. And then it's going to be Billy's turn. I promised him.'

While all this was going on Elfie went inside to fetch her bag. She would stay overnight in Hampstead and her father would bring her back in the morning on his way to work and collect Joe at the same time.

When she came back out Ivy was in the process of getting out of the car and Elfie's father was asking Mabel if she'd like a ride next but she was shaking her head. She was afraid of motor cars. She didn't trust them not to crash. A driver could always bring a horse to a stop, she said. But what if the motor in the car failed?

Then, to Elfie's horror, Gertie stepped forward. 'I'd like a ride if yez please, mister.'

'Step in, young lady.' Elfie's father held the passenger door open and bowed her in.

'Steady now.' Joe put a hand on Elfie's arm.

Gertie swivelled round to meet Elfie's eyes. She waved and then the motor car roared into action and they were off up Green Lanes.

'How nice of your father to give everyone a treat,' observed Pa Bigsby.

Elfie said nothing. She might just explode. Gertie was sitting in *her* seat. She didn't mind Joe or Billy or any of the others, even Ivy, sitting in it, but Gertie!

'That were great,' said Gertie, when they arrived back. She sat on in the passenger seat, in no hurry to move. 'I could sit 'ere all day in this lovely motor car.'

Elfie glared at her but Gertie was not even looking in her direction. She was smiling at Elfie's father.

Pa Bigsby came to the rescue. 'Time to get out now, Gertie. Mr Trelawney will want to be on his way.'

'I'm afraid I can't take you with us, dear,' said Elfie's father to Gertie. 'Perhaps another day.'

Take Gertie with them! Elfie would soon knock that idea on the head.

'Ta very much, mister,' said Gertie, as Elfie's father helped her out. 'I'm ever so grateful.'

He turned to Elfie. 'Ready then, love?'

She couldn't wait to go.

※◦⊙◦⊱

Ethel, the maid, opened the door to them. She was wearing her usual black dress, white frilly apron and a black and white hat. Henry, the butler, had Sundays off, as did Mrs Munn, the housekeeper, so that Elfie only saw them occasionally. Cook worked on Sundays so that she could cook the roast.

When Elfie had first come she'd been amazed at the number of staff in the house with only three people to look after. Plus Rosalind's Nanny too, of course. They could have done with some of them to help out at the *Pig and Whistle*. When Elfie had commented on that to her father he'd been a bit embarrassed. He'd said that Clarissa – that was his wife – was used to living in style as she had come from a well-off family. Landed gentry, he'd called them. His own family had been in the timber business and had lived more modestly, with only one cook-housekeeper. Clarissa's parents had not considered him to be a good match for their daughter, even if he was a qualified lawyer. The problem was that he had come from what they referred to as "trade". Elfie had never met them and hoped she never would. But she thought Clarissa must have been madly in love with her father to go against their wishes.

'Good morning, Miss Elfie,' said Ethel, giving her a slight curtsey. 'Miss Rosalind's waiting for you.'

Elfie had given up asking Ethel to drop the "Miss" and the curtsey. Rosalind said it was only right and proper that Ethel should address her in the correct way since she was a servant and Elfie a member of the family. Her mother would insist on it.

Rosalind appeared at the top of stairs.

'Elfie, you're late! Hurry up! I've got something to show you.'

'Hang on, Rosalind,' said their father. 'And don't be so bossy! Let Elfie get her breath back.'

But Elfie could cope with Rosalind's bossiness.

They walked up the wide curving staircase. The walls on either side were lined with large gold-framed paintings of old-fashioned people. Clarissa's ancestors. Elfie thought they all looked very dull. Not a smile creased any of their faces.

Mrs Trelawney had by now joined Rosalind on the top landing.

'How lovely to see you, dear.' She came forward to kiss Elfie on the cheek. She smelled of lily of the valley. She, like Rosalind, had golden hair and a pink and white complexion. No one would ever have taken the two girls for sisters, even half-sisters, with Elfie being so dark and Rosalind so fair. Elfie had heard Cook discussing it with Mrs Munn in the kitchen one day. Elfie of course took after her father and Mrs Munn had said she wouldn't be one bit surprised if he didn't have a touch of the tar brush in his blood. Their voices had dropped for the rest of the conversation.

Clarissa Trelawney was a nice woman and Elfie liked her even if she couldn't imagine ever calling her Mother as her father hoped she might one day. She called him Papa, the same as Rosalind did. It was what he wanted.

'I think Cook should be ready to serve shortly,' said Mrs Trelawney. 'Would you like to go to your room and change first, Elfie?'

She liked Elfie to take off her *Pig and Whistle* clothes when she arrived and put on ones that she had chosen specially for her. Elfie didn't mind. She liked dressing up. She found an emerald green velvet dress laid out on the bed with white lace stockings and a pair of black patent shoes placed neatly together on the floor. It was as if she became a different person when she changed her clothes, like Alice through the looking glass. She pirouetted in front of the long oval mirror.

'My name is Elfrieda Trelawney,' she said to her image. And then she giggled.

In the hall below Ethel banged the gong.

Rosalind poked her nose around the door. 'Are you coming, Elfie?'

The dining room was on the ground floor. The table was set with a white cloth and gleaming silver cutlery, like the one in the restaurant. Ethel brought the soup in a large tureen, which she set in the middle of the table. The master of the house served, and so the meal commenced.

Elfie enjoyed the food well enough but she was glad when it was over as Mrs Trelawney kept asking her questions. Were Mr and Mrs Bigsby well? What book were they reading in their Literature class? How had she been entertaining herself all week? As if Elfie could begin to tell her! Mrs Trelawney had never been to the *Pig and Whistle*. She had no reason to go anywhere near Stoke Newington.

'You are happy there still, dear?' she asked.

'Yes, thank you,' said Elfie.

When they were permitted to leave the table Elfie and Rosalind escaped upstairs to Rosalind's room. She had a new doll, with golden hair and a pink and white complexion.

'Oh no!' Elfie made a face. 'You've got enough of them dolls. They're all the same. Look at them!'

They were all lined up in a row against the wall.

Rosalind pouted. 'But this one's got a red dress. I thought you'd like it. I was going to ask you to give her a name.'

'What about Rapunzel?'

'That's a funny name.'

'There's a fairytale about her. I'll tell it to you.'

After she'd heard the story of Rapunzel and her hair that grew so long she could let it down over the castle ramparts Rosalind agreed with Elfie's suggestion.

'Do you think my dolly's hair will grow?'

'It might if you call her Rapunzel.'

Elfie remembered she'd left her bag in the hall. She told Rosalind she was going to nip down to fetch it.

The dining room door was ajar and her father and Mrs Trelawney were still in there, sitting over their coffee. They were talking.

Elfie knew it was wrong to eavesdrop but there were times when she just couldn't help it. Her ear had caught the word "money".

'We're spending too much money, Clarissa.' That was what her father had said. He'd sounded worried too.

'We can't go on like this. Even the party last night cost a fair bit. I didn't need it for my birthday.'

'But, Alfred, I wanted you to have something special to celebrate your birthday.'

'Not if we can't afford it.'

'I thought things were better now that you've taken Mr Basildon-Blunt on as a partner?'

'It's more like he's taken me on.'

'Do you mean he is trying to be the lead partner?'

'Yes.' The answer was so quiet that Elfie just caught it. She moved a step closer.

'You can't allow that, Alfred! Why should you?'

'It's complicated, dear. I can't go into details.'

'It's outrageous! I must have a word with Papa. I'm sure he will know someone at his club who can sort out your Mr Basildon-Blunt. I have to confess I did not care for the man when you introduced us.'

'No, Clarissa, please don't say a word to your father! I can sort this out myself. But we shall have to cut down on our spending, I'm afraid. Drastically.'

'But, Alfred, what can we cut down on?' cried Clarissa. 'We only have one maid, one cook, one butler, one coachman, one nanny! We can't do without any of them.'

'I suppose not. Doesn't Cook have a scullery maid to help her too?'

'She needs her! She would probably leave if we were to dismiss Beryl. Besides, that would only save pennies.'

Why couldn't Clarissa do the cooking herself? Elfie wondered. It would give her something to do with herself instead of embroidering tray cloths and having her lady friends to tea. Or they could get rid of Nanny since Rosalind went to day school now. And in a year or two, when she turned nine, she was due to go to boarding school. Her mother thought the company would be good for her. Elfie was inclined to agree with her there. Rosalind was always begging her to come and live with them.

'What can we cut down on?' asked Clarissa again.

'I'm afraid we can't go to Italy this summer.'

'But, Alfred, I've so been looking forward to it! That villa up on the hill outside Florence is simply delightful. You will love it, I promise you. I remember an absolutely wonderful summer there when I was a child. Father rented it for three months.'

'I've just cancelled it, Clarissa. I'm sorry. I truly am.'

'*Cancelled* it? Without consulting me?'

There was going to be a row now, thought Elfie.

And there was. It ended with Clarissa leaving the room and running up the stairs sobbing. Elfie imagined her going into her bedroom and flinging herself face downwards on the bed.

Elfie's father emerged from the dining room looking so unhappy that she wanted to go and throw her arms around him. But if she were to do that he might guess she'd been eavesdropping.

'I just came down for my bag.' She picked it up.

'Would you like to go for a walk on the heath?'

'Love to.'

'Better see if Rosalind would like to come too. It would do her good to take some exercise. I fear she doesn't get enough.'

As a result Rosalind was a little plump. But Elfie could not persuade her to go for a walk. It was far too cold outside. She was miffed when Elfie said she was going anyway. Elfie left her to sulk, after promising that she'd read to her when she came back.

They didn't talk much, Elfie and her father, as they walked across the heath. She could see he was sorely troubled but knew that he would not want her to ask questions. She would wait and discuss it with Joe tomorrow when she was back at the *Pig and Whistle*.

≈≈≈≈

Elfie did not see Mrs Trelawney again that day.

Ethel came into the drawing room when it was time for afternoon tea to announce that Madam would not be coming down to join them. She said it a bit smugly, Elfie thought, as if she knew that her father and his wife had had a row. Of course, with the dining room door ajar, the whole house could have heard.

The low round table had already been set with a silver teapot and hot water jug, fine china cups, saucers and plates. Ethel now set down a three-tiered stand that had little triangular sandwiches on the top deck, buttered tea bread on the second, and cream cakes on the bottom. After asking if there would be anything else, she withdrew.

'We might as well start then,' said Alfred Trelawney, trying to sound cheerful, and failing.

He drank a cup of tea, that was all. Elfie and Rosalind demolished the dainty sandwiches, skipped the tea bread and ate all the cream cakes. Ethel and Cook would eat up the tea bread, said Rosalind. Elfie couldn't help thinking they could save some money in the house by buying less food. That's what Ma Bigsby would say. She knew where to buy cheap cuts of meat and she was a dab hand when it came to haggling over prices on the market stalls. She could give Mrs Trelawney and Cook a tip or two. Ma said she had to make the money spin out, with so many mouths to feed.

Elfie went to bed that night with her stomach feeling like an overstuffed cushion. She lay awake for a while thinking about her father and his problems. Old Blunt-Face was giving him a hard time at work, and his wife at home. From his troubles she moved to her own. She only had one. That was enough. Gertie!

Mrs Trelawney didn't come down for breakfast next morning either. But then she never did. She breakfasted in bed. Nanny was back by that time to get Rosalind ready for school. Swain would drive them in the carriage.

Elfie walked around to the garage with her father.

'Is Mrs Trelawney all right?' she asked.

'She's fine, thank you, Elfie.'

'I was wondering if her headache had gone?'

'Not quite. But I expect she'll be as right as rain if she rests today.'

But she seemed to rest every day. Elfie would have thought she'd be bored to death. Ma Bigsby said Elfie shouldn't judge the woman, she'd been brought up that way and knew no other. Ma herself was up at six every morning and after a mug of strong tea would be singing about Molly Malone and her wheelbarrow.

Swain had been polishing up the car until its long black bonnet shone. Alfred Trelawney complimented the coachman.

'Thank you, sir.' Swain touched his cap. 'Shall I crank up the engine for you?'

'Yes, please, Swain.'

Elfie got in beside her father and they were soon on their way to Stoke Newington, weaving through the buses and horse-drawn carts. They made good time to the *Pig and Whistle*.

As usual, the sound of the car engine alerted Billy. He was always first out onto the pavement.

Today, though, he was closely followed by Ivy.

'You'll never guess,' she cried to Elfie across the pavement. She had news and was bursting to tell it.

'What? What's happened?'

'Gertie's done a bunk!'

Chapter Seven:
A Station Rendezvous

'Done a bunk?' repeated Elfie.

'Went last night,' said Ivy, who was enjoying telling the news. 'Took off while we was sleeping.'

'Were,' corrected Elfie. It was getting to be second nature for her, correcting other people's speech, like it was with Joe. Not that she always remembered to use the right word herself! Her grammar wavered at times, especially when she felt excited, which she did just now. Could it be *true*? That Gertie had gone of her own free will?

'Must have went at dead of night,' continued Ivy. 'Not one of us heard a sound. You didn't, did you, Billy?' He shook his head. 'She stole two half-crowns and a shilling from Ma's purse – that were all that was in it.' The purse usually sat on the high shelf in the kitchen. 'Took the blanket off her bed and all and a ham from the larder. Ma had just cooked it that arternoon.'

'Did she go in the clothes Ma gave her?'

Ivy nodded. 'And the coat with the fur collar.'

'I can't understand why she'd want to leave,' said Billy.

Elfie could. When she'd first come to the *Pig and Whistle* she'd felt shut in by walls. It had taken a while for her to get used to spending so much of the day inside. There were times even now when she felt tempted to take off and run free for a few hours, but Ma wouldn't go for that. And she knew Ma talked sense when she said you had to have a daily routine with thirteen of them living in the house.

At least now there would not be fourteen! That was a relief.

'Good riddance to bad rubbish is wot I sez,' declared Ivy.

'Me too,' agreed Elfie fervently. It seemed too good to be true.

'She tried to nick my necklace, the one with the blue stones. You know the one that Florrie give me for Christmas? I caught her at it.'

Elfie sympathised. For once she was on Ivy's side!

Joe appeared in the doorway wearing his business clothes. Every time Elfie saw him she wanted to giggle and had to bite it back. He could tell from her face though what she was thinking.

'You look ever so smart, Joe,' she said. 'No, honest you do.'

'Extremely,' added Elfie's father, who was also dressed for the office, though he wore a frock coat and carried a black top hat that he donned whenever he had to go out and call on a client. Otherwise, he preferred to go bareheaded. Elfie couldn't abide hats either.

'Shall we get on our way then, Joe?'

Billy and the two girls waved them off. Elfie wished she was going with them. She sighed, picked up her bag and followed Ivy and Billy into the house. At least Gertie wouldn't be sitting in there crowing.

Ma and Pa Bigsby were both in the kitchen. Ma was drinking tea, which she did at intervals throughout the day. She said it kept her afloat to cope with the vicissitudes of life. She'd got that word from Pa. He was reading *The Times*.

'Her Royal Highness is sinking,' he announced. 'God bless her soul.'

Elfie had more interesting things to talk about. 'Ivy's been telling me about Gertie and what she took.'

'It was a lovely ham.' Ma shook her head. 'Prime pork. The best.'

'Will you be setting Dowdy on her, Pa?' asked Elfie.

He looked at her over the edge of his newspaper. He wore a monocle attached to a purple ribbon when he was reading.

'Dowdy is not a dog.'

'No, but he's good at catching criminals.'

'I don't know that I care to classify Gertie as a criminal.'

'But that's what she is! She stole a whole lot of money from Ma, and a ham and a good blanket. It was nearly new, wasn't it, Ma?'

Ma merely sighed and took another mouthful of tea.

'You're not going to let her off with it, are you?' Elfie was incensed.

'You can't, Pa,' cried Ivy. 'She should go to the gaol. There was a girl wot used to live in Florrie's boarding house who stole arf a crown and got sent to Holloway.'

'I would not wish that on any young child.' Pa removed his eye monocle. 'Or woman, either. The conditions are appalling, fit for neither man nor beast.' He belonged to some kind of action committee that campaigned for prison reform.

'Wot if she was a murderer?' Ivy was scandalised.

'Gertie may have her faults but I hardly think she is that.'

'She could be,' said Elfie.

'Let us not allow our imaginations to run away with us! Gertie took a few things when she left and I have no doubt she will have need of them, especially since it is the dead of winter.'

'Poor child.' Ma sighed again.

'Ma!' cried Elfie and Ivy simultaneously.

'Yes, poor child,' said Pa. He could be very irritating at times. 'She is to be pitied. Now off you go and get ready for class. The first lesson this morning will be trigonometry.'

'All those angles again,' groaned Elfie.

'There may come a time when you might be glad to know the difference between an acute and a right angle.'

Elfie couldn't imagine it but Pa knew more than she

did, a lot more, so she could only take his word for it. Anyway, there would be no escaping this thing called trigonometry.

At least, after lunch, she and Billy would be off out on their delivery rounds while Ivy would be sewing lace on pillowslips. That was something to be thankful for.

※※(づ)※※

On Wednesday afternoon they had fewer errands so they finished quickly that day. There was plenty of time left before tea for Billy to pay a visit to King's Cross station. Elfie said she would go with him. They got a lift with Tommy, who offered to pick them up on his way back. Elfie liked railway stations herself. There was always something going on, with trains arriving from all over the place and people coming and going.

She hadn't bargained on seeing Mr Reginald Basildon-Blunt, though, and for a moment she didn't recognise him. He was wearing a grey bowler, rather than a top hat, and a long grey coat that covered his lawyer's clothes. Elfie started when she saw him enter the station and begin to weave his way through the crowds towards the platforms. He hadn't noticed her, he was too intent on where he was going, and the throng of travellers was too thick. She couldn't help herself. She got off her bench and followed.

He seemed not to be travelling himself. He carried no case. After consulting the Arrivals Board he walked towards the platforms and stopped at a barrier. He had a few words with one of the station employees, then he began to pace up and down. He took his watch from his pocket. He frowned. The train he was expecting must be late. Elfie looked up at the station clock. The hands stood at half past three. Who was Blunt-Face going to meet? A man or a woman? A sweetheart? Elfie couldn't imagine him having one of those. She went a little closer to get a better view.

Suddenly there was action. A train was approaching the platform. The chugging noise of its engine filled the air. Smoke billowed upwards. Porters hurried, trundling their barrows.

Basildon-Blunt moved nearer the barrier. He glanced over his shoulder and Elfie ducked behind a large woman carrying a huge basket over each fat arm. The baskets were full of dead rabbits.

A family came through the barrier; a man and a woman with five children in their wake, like ducklings in a line. Basildon-Blunt was not interested in them. He was craning his neck. Next came two young women, arm-in-arm, wearing wide feathered hats. They were talking and laughing. Two elderly women emerged, followed by three men in business outfits walking as if late for appointments, then another family and yet another and a couple who seemed to be in love. They were holding hands and smiling at each other and taking their time. Basildon-Blunt was looking impatient. Perhaps the person he was meeting had missed the train.

Then Blunt-Face relaxed. A man was coming through

the barrier whom he recognised. They nodded at each other but did not shake hands. Odd, thought Elfie. Her father and Pa Bigsby shook hands with nearly everybody they met. Basildon-Blunt turned and made his way back out through the station trailed a few feet behind by the unknown man. Elfie went too.

The man wore a fawn mackintosh and a black bowler. He did not look like a lawyer. He did not look like the kind of man whom Basildon-Blunt would befriend.

They walked a little way down Euston Road and went into a café, a workman's café, called the *Euston Cocoa Rooms*. It was quite different from the *Vienna Café* in Oxford Street that Elfie's father took her to sometimes. Her papa knew a lot of good coffee houses where he liked to drink coffee and read the newspapers. She pulled her hood over her head to conceal part of her face and strolled slowly past the café window. Basildon-Blunt and his companion were sitting at the back of the room. It was not large and there were few other customers so she had a clear view of them. They were facing each other over a narrow table. She saw her father's partner pass something – an envelope, she thought – over to the other man, who slipped it into his coat pocket without even looking inside. Curiouser and curiouser. She loved that phrase from *Alice in Wonderland*. Pa Bigsby had read it to them before Christmas. She went into a shop doorway nearby and waited.

It was not long before the two men came out. After exchanging a brief word they parted, the unknown man to head back towards King's Cross and Basildon-Blunt to hail a cab. He had not noticed Elfie, she was convinced of that.

She scurried after the other man into the station and saw him go into the Gentlemen's lavatory. She hovered. When he reappeared she tailed him again and halfway across the concourse she pretended to slip and managed to bump into him sideways on. He swivelled round and grabbed her by the arm, as if he thought she was trying to pickpocket him.

'Watch what you're doing, miss!'

'Sorry, sir! I'm really ever so sorry.' Elfie released her arm. 'I slipped. I couldn't help it. Somebody must have spilt something.'

'Best keep your eyes on the ground in future!'

'Oh yes, indeed, sir, I will,' she said. She was keeping her eyes on the man's face so that she would know it again. It was long and narrow and his eyelids drooped.

He hurried on without giving her another glance. She didn't think he would know her again for he had not looked her in the face. He had patted his pocket, the one containing the envelope, as if to make sure it was still there. She watched him as he headed back towards the platform where he had arrived a short time earlier. His stay in London had been very short but it must have been important for him to come so far. She wished she could have found out what was in the envelope. It irked her not to know. If Gertie had been there she would have picked his pocket in a flash. She was skilled in the business. Elfie, however, was thankful that she had not been there.

'Elfie!' Billy was yelling at her and waving. 'Where've you bin? I bin lookin' for you all over. Tommy's waitin' for us. Git a move on!'

'Coming!' She ran to join him.

She didn't tell Billy about the man but she could scarcely wait to tell Joe. She hung around in the street when his bus was due. A fog had descended all of a sudden and was hanging over Green Lanes, blurring the street lamps and chilling the evening air. People loomed up out of the mist like ghostly creatures. The women humped bags of shopping and trailed kids behind them. The men were coming back from work. They trudged with their heads down, caps pulled low over their foreheads.

A few dropped into the *Pig* for a glass of stout on their way home. Ma said some came in to get warm and she didn't blame them. The ones without a family tended to live in single unheated rooms. She kept the fire stoked high in the bar.

Sad Sid arrived. He spent his evenings in the pub, toasting his feet at the coals.

'You'll catch yer death out there,' he told Elfie. 'It's an 'orrible night.'

'Horrible,' she said. 'How're you doing?'

He leaned towards her. 'You know me greatest fear, Elfie?'

'No.'

'That I'll end a pauper. In the workhouse at Islington.'

'Meg'll see you don't.' She was at least ten years younger than Sid.

'If she comes lookin' for me tell her you've not seen sight of me.'

He pushed open the bar door, letting out a stream of light and a gust of laughter and then he disappeared inside.

Elfie hopped about on the pavement to keep warm. Carriages and carts rolled past. And then she saw the lamps of a bus looming up through the gloom. She ran to the stop as the bus pulled up and Joe alighted. The moment he had his feet on the pavement she spilled out her news.

'Curiouser and curiouser,' he said, making her laugh.

Chapter Eight:
The Stalking of Mr
Basildon-Blunt

Elfie was allowed to go into town on Saturday and meet Joe after he finished work. There were no lessons and no chores on Saturday afternoons. It was free time for the older children, as long as they told Ma Bigsby where they were going and what they were doing. Mabel and Ivy had arranged to visit an elderly great-aunt of Mabel's who lived in Camden Town and seemed to have endless supplies of fly cemeteries and iced biscuits with a cherry on top. Ivy always came back bragging about how many she'd eaten.

No one needed to ask where Billy would be heading.

Elfie arrived punctually in Chancery Lane, a few minutes before twelve, carrying a bag, empty save for a blue muffler, as requested by Joe. She was admitted to the waiting room by Parker, who looked down his nose and sniffed as usual.

'Have you got a cold?' asked Elfie.

He gave her a haughty look and retreated. She made a face at the closed door.

Shortly afterwards, her father came into the room and she ran into his arms to give him a hug.

'I hear you and Joe plan to spend the afternoon in town? What will you do? Visit Hyde Park? Or go to the museum? The Victoria and Albert?'

'We might.' It was unlikely, however. They had other, more urgent, things to do. 'I'm not sure if we'll have time.'

'You'll have plenty of time. It stays open until ten!'

Her father took a coin from his pocket and put it in her hand. 'Here, take this! Go to a café and have something to eat and drink.'

She looked at the half-crown lying in her palm. 'But, Papa, that's too much!' Ma Bigsby could probably cook a meal of tripe and onions with treacle pudding to follow for that amount of money – and have sixpence left over. And that would be for thirteen of them. Elfie was thinking, too, of how worried her father had sounded about money. She didn't want to make it any worse for him. Joe was certain that he was in debt to Basildon-Blunt. Last night he'd told Elfie that he'd overheard the latter say something about a payment being overdue and that he was not prepared to wait much longer. Joe said it would have been difficult not to hear. Blunt-Face had been shouting.

Elfie's father coloured slightly, as if he knew what was running through her mind. 'If you have a shilling or so in change keep it for a treat another time.'

'Thank you, Papa. You are very kind to me.' She gave him another hug.

'I have eleven years to make up for, don't I? Before I found you?' He smiled.

The door opened to admit Joe ready for the street. He was wearing his coat and carrying his hat. He really did hate that hat. He would have loved to toss it into the river and watch it float away downstream. His thick black curly hair was enough protection from the cold.

'I've finished those letters, Mr Trelawney.'

'Excellent, Joe! I'll read them over on Monday. I'm about to leave myself. I'll walk out with you.'

They parted from him on the pavement outside. He kissed Elfie and told Joe that he would see him on Monday morning, outside the *Pig*, when he brought Elfie back. He had got into the habit that everyone else had of calling the Bigsbys' establishment the *Pig*. Mrs Trelawney didn't like it. Rosalind was convinced they had a real live pig in the house and that it could blow a whistle. She was dying to come for a visit but her mother was not keen.

'Sometime, dear,' she would say vaguely when Rosalind pressed her.

Elfie and Joe crossed the road and walked a short way up Carey Street, where they stopped. Joe undid his tie and wrenched off his starched collar then handed both over to Elfie along with his bowler. She put them all in the bag and gave him the muffler, which he wound around his neck.

'That's better.' He heaved a sigh of relief.

They then hurried back to the end of the street from where they would have a good view of the lawyers' door. Joe knew that Mr Reginald Basildon-Blunt would cut across to Fetter Lane on his way home for he had watched him go that way on several occasions. Joe also reckoned that he must live close by since he walked to the office daily.

They saw the door open and the lawyer come out, wearing his top hat. He nodded to Parker, who was holding the door for him, and set off at brisk pace down a side street as Joe had predicted. They followed at a distance. Should he turn round there would be no milling crowds to skulk behind as there had been in the railway station. But if he did see them he would probably think they were on their way home. Why should he imagine they were following him?

'Unless he has something to hide,' said Joe. 'And I'm fairly sure he does. He gives me suspicious looks all the time. He wants rid of me, I know that.'

'Papa wouldn't allow it.'

'Come on!' Joe led the way.

Moving cautiously, keeping several yards behind, they continued in pursuit of their quarry. He carried on a little way up Fetter Lane, then he turned left into Norwich Street. At the corner he came to a halt in front of a house, stepped up to the door, opened it and disappeared inside.

'So that must be his house,' said Joe.

'Now what do we do?'

'Well, if we were police, and had a suspect, we would keep him under surveillance.'

'What does that mean?'

'Watch him.'

'You and Pa Bigsby and your big words!'

'We like words.'

'But how can we watch him when he's inside the house and the door's shut?'

'We can wait and see if he comes out again.'

'But he might stay in there the whole afternoon.' Waiting did not hold much appeal for Elfie. Tracking Blunt-Face and his friend around King's Cross station and along Euston Road had been much more exciting. She was beginning to wish, too, that she had brought some bread and cheese in the bag. She fingered the half-crown in her pocket but there were no cafés round about.

Joe had reason though to think that Blunt-Face might not remain inside. They had installed a telephone in the office and he had overheard Basildon-Blunt making an arrangement to call on someone that afternoon. His door had been slightly ajar.

'He said he'd see him – whoever he is – at two o'clock.'

'Did he say where?'

'No, but I got the impression that it wasn't too far away. I'm hoping he'll go on foot. If he takes a bus or a carriage we're sunk.'

They retraced their steps to a cul-de-sac called Plough

Place. It seemed a good enough place to wait. There was no sign of life at any of the houses. Elfie dumped her bag on the pavement and perched on a low wall. Joe paced a few steps up and down, keeping an eye on the entrance to Norwich Street.

'This is like being Sherlock Holmes, isn't it?' said Elfie. Pa Bigsby had finished reading 'The Adventure of the Speckled Band' and they were about to start on 'A Scandal in Bohemia'. None of the stories were very long.

'Not quite. Sherlock Holmes doesn't go out sleuthing or following suspects round the streets. He sits in his rooms smoking his pipe and thinking, and people come to him with their problems.'

'I wouldn't mind being a detective when I grow up.'

'You'd have to learn patience!'

Joe grinned and ducked as Elfie tried to take a swipe at him.

She was beginning to get restless when a loud irate voice hailed them. There was no mistaking the anger in it.

'What the devil are you two up to?'

Elfie and Joe wheeled round. The voice belonged to a police constable, who was running towards them, bristling with anger, his helmet bobbing from side to side.

'Oh, Lor'!' said Elfie

'Stay calm,' murmured Joe.

'Well now, what would the two of you be doing here?' The constable was red in the face and breathing heavily through his nostrils. 'Up to no good, I'll be bound.'

He was too fat for running, thought Elfie, but she'd better not tell him that or he'd hit the ceiling. She was tempted but resisted. Instead she put on an innocent little girl's voice, one she'd had occasion to use in the past.

'We ain't doing nothing, sir. We was just resting.'

'Resting, is it?' The constable was more interested in Joe. 'Loitering is what I'd call it. Loitering with intent.'

'Intent to do what?' asked Elfie, who couldn't keep the innocent voice going for long.

'Whatever opportunities comes your way.' He was still eyeing Joe. 'Folks round here don't want the likes of you hanging about. Scum!'

'How dare you!' cried Elfie. 'He works for my pa.'

'What's he then, eh? A fence?'

'He's a lawyer.'

'And mine's the Duke of York!' The constable had a disgusting laugh. He took hold of Joe by the coat collar with both hands and looked him straight in the face. 'I suggest you move on, darkie, before I charges you.'

Joe had gone rigid. His eyes were huge and full of anguish. Elfie knew he could defend himself, but he wouldn't. He could flatten the constable with a couple of punches but he wouldn't dare. He'd end up in Newgate Gaol.

But Elfie had no such qualms. She flew at the policeman. 'Take your hands off him!'

The constable turned and shoved Elfie hard. She fell backwards, catching the side of her head on a railing.

'You've hurt her!' Joe was angry now. He shook himself free and bent down to help Elfie up. He took a large white handkerchief from his pocket and held it against her forehead to stem the flow of blood.

'She's bleeding,' he said unnecessarily.

'Any more of your cheek and I'll sort the two of you out.' The constable took the baton from his waist and let it swing loosely by his side. His eyes narrowed. 'And I ain't joking.'

'Her father is a lawyer.' Joe kept his voice level. 'His name is Mr Alfred Trelawney and his chambers are nearby in Chancery Lane. You may go and check. His brass plate is on the door.'

'And Joe is his clerk,' added Elfie. 'His right-hand man.'

She wanted to tell the constable to put that in his pipe and smoke it but thought better of that too. She'd give him something to think about though.

'He'll be furious when he sees what you've done to me,' she carried on. 'He knows *all* the judges in London and he has a friend who is a top police inspector at Scotland Yard. And one of *our* best friends is a policeman in Stoke Newington. Constable O'Dowd's his name. Wait till he hears about it! He'll be raging.' The last bit at least was accurate.

The constable was looking less sure of himself now.

'It's not a good idea to hang about the streets,' he muttered. 'That way you ask for trouble.'

'We're not asking for any trouble,' retorted Elfie. 'We were resting. I told you.'

The policeman spun around on his heel and went off without another word. But before he turned the corner he spat on the ground.

'Scum yourself!' Elfie shouted after him.

Joe shook his head.

'Well, he is!'

'Are you all right?' Joe's voice was full of anxiety.

He was more troubled about the encounter than she was. She had been confronted by nasty coppers before in her life, though not for a year or more. Living at the *Pig* protected you from such things, most of the time anyway, and especially in their part of Stoke Newington where everybody knew them and Dowdy patrolled the streets.

'It's only a little cut. I'll be right as rain in a minute. Hey, why is rain right? Why not sunshine?'

'Don't know.'

'I thought you knewed everything.' Elfie grinned. She was winding Joe up. Pa Bigsby had told her recently that her use of language was much improved.

'*Knew*. Well, I don't! I wish I did.'

'We'll need to ask Pa Bigsby.'

Joe pulled out his watch.

'What's the time?'

'Twenty to two! We must go! I hope we haven't missed him.'

They ran to the corner and peered around just in time

to see Basildon-Blunt nearing the top of Fetter Lane. They took to their heels and pelted after him. He was still in their sights when they reached the main road. He had crossed over and was turning up Leather Lane. He had changed his clothes for the grey coat and bowler he'd worn at King's Cross.

They followed now at a more measured pace, set by Joe. They took the opposite side of the street and kept to the inside of the pavement, close to the walls.

'Wait!' Joe pulled Elfie back into a doorway.

Basildon-Blunt had slowed his step. He now came to a halt outside a leather goods shop. He turned to take a look around, then entered. Elfie wondered what he would buy there.

'Maybe nothing.' Joe was watching intently.

After ten minutes there was still no sign of Basildon-Blunt. They couldn't make out anything of the interior of the shop.

'We could walk past and take a quick peek in,' suggested Elfie.

'And bump into him coming out!' Joe shook his head. 'Let's wait a bit.'

Elfie sighed. Her stomach was rumbling, telling her it needed help. Joe was so much more patient than she was.

'Another customer going in,' he commented. 'Interesting.'

The man was wearing a mackintosh and a flat cap. From what Joe could see in the shop window, the goods on sale, leather trunks and saddle bags, looked as if they would be expensive. It was not the kind of shop you'd expect that man to patronise.

Fifteen more minutes passed and neither the lawyer nor the man in the cap had reappeared.

'Joe, if you stay here I could nip past the door quick as greased lightning,' said Elfie. 'It's a glass door, ain't it?'

'The top half is.'

'All right?'

Joe nodded. He knew he couldn't do it himself. He would be too noticeable and Elfie was fast on her feet.

She darted over to the other side of the road, weaving her way between a carriage and a cart, causing the driver of the latter to raise his fist and curse her. As she neared the leather shop she quickened her pace and turned her head to the side. Going past she had a clear view of the door and the interior. There was nobody inside. On the door hung a sign saying CLOSED.

She rushed back to report to Joe.

'Where can they be?'

'There's a flat over the shop.' Joe looked up. 'Net curtains, so I can't see anything. They must be up there. Let's hang on a bit longer.'

They had only five minutes to wait before the door opened and the man in the cap came out. He crossed the road and began to walk in their direction.

'Don't worry,' said Joe. 'He doesn't know us. He can't.'

They moved further back into the recess of the doorway.

The man passed them by, looking straight ahead.

Elfie frowned and leaned out to peer after him. 'I've seen that man before, I'm sure I have.' But she couldn't think where.

'Keep in!' urged Joe. 'Blunt-Face is coming out now.'

Basildon-Blunt had stopped on the pavement outside the shop to put on his bowler and button up his coat. Then he set off back along the road.

'Will we go after him?' asked Elfie.

Joe didn't think there would be much point in doing that. 'He'll very likely go on home. No, we should have followed the other man but it's too late for that now.'

He was gone, around the corner, out of sight.

'Did you notice anything about Blunt-Face?' asked Joe. 'Anything different from before he went into the shop?'

'No, what do you mean?'

'His coat pocket was bulging.'

'Bulging?'

'His left-hand pocket. The one next to the street. I think he must have put something in there while he was in the shop.'

'Not a leather bag!'

'Hardly! His pocket wasn't big enough for that.'

'But when he walked up the street you'd have seen his other pocket, wouldn't you? The one on the right-hand side!' Elfie felt pleased with herself for thinking of that. Maybe she could be a detective.

'But he turned around outside the shop, remember?

I could swear he had nothing bulky in either pocket then.'

'Joe, you've got eyes as sharp as tacks. You could be a policeman!'

'They wouldn't have me.'

No, they probably wouldn't. Elfie didn't argue with him about that. 'Anyhow, you're going to be a lawyer one of these days.'

'We'll see.'

'Pa Bigsby says you've got to have faith in yourself.' He told them all that.

Joe was thinking about the men. 'They're up to something, the two them. The question is what?'

'I'm starving,' moaned Elfie. 'And I've got half a crown in my pocket.'

They found a café on the main road and had sausages and mash and a mug of tea.

'Thank goodness,' said Elfie, sitting back, when she'd finished the last bite. Ma always said she didn't know where she put all the food she ate. Not on her bones anyway!

Time was moving on. They had to get home to help with the preparations for Saturday night at the *Pig*. Nothing could be allowed to interfere with that.

The bar was full, and Ma was just opening up on 'Molly Malone', when Elfie remembered where she had seen the man in the flat cap.

Chapter Nine:
Links in the Chain

'Down at the docks,' shouted Elfie across the crowded room to Joe, who was picking up dirty glasses from the tables.

'*In Dublin's fair city,*' sang Ma. '*Where the girls are so pretty . . .*'

Joe shook his head at Elfie. He couldn't make out a word she'd said. The customers were joining in. The noise level was soaring.

'*I first set my eyes on sweet Molly Malone*
'*As she wheeled her wheelbarrow through streets broad and narrow . . .*'

When they reached the chorus they sang with extra gusto and swayed from side to side. You couldn't even hear yourself think then.

'*A-live a-live O! A-live a-live O!*
'*Crying cockles and mussels,*
'*Alive-a-live-O!*'

It was a great tune but Elfie found it odd that the song should be so popular when poor old Molly dies of a fever in the end, like her mother and father before her. Elfie wondered if Ma Bigsby had ever wheeled a wheelbarrow with cockles and mussels through the streets of Dublin before she'd come to London and met Pa Bigsby. From the way she sang it you'd think she had.

Joe had filled the big round tray with glasses and was carrying it through to the back scullery. Elfie went after him.

'That man,' she said excitedly. 'I remember now where I saw him.'

'You do? Where?'

'Down at the docks.'

'The *docks*? Are you sure?'

'I could swear on it! What's more, I have a funny feeling that's where I saw Blunt-Face one time. Only he was wearing an old mac and a flat cap.'

'What's this about docks?' asked Pa Bigsby, coming up behind them. 'You've not been down there, I hope?'

'No, Pa, we wasn't.'

'Weren't,' said Joe.

'You know they're out of bounds?'

'Yes, Pa,' said Elfie in a meek voice, which did not fool Pa.

He gave her a stern look. 'I hope you do. What were you doing this afternoon anyway? Where did you go?'

'We walked about.' He didn't seem satisfied with

that for an answer so Elfie added, 'We sort of looked at the shop windows and things.' That didn't convince him, either.

'I understood that you intended to visit a museum? The Victoria and Albert? Did you not mention it, Joe?'

'Well, yes.' Joe concentrated on putting the glasses into the sink. 'We might go next Saturday.'

'Papa gave me half a crown so we went to a café and had sausages and mash.' Elfie rattled on, 'The café was all right, wasn't it, Joe? It was dead clean. Even Ma couldn't have found any fault with the floors and the sausages were good.'

So what was wrong with that? After all, Ivy and Mabel had spent the afternoon stuffing themselves with biscuits and Pa hadn't suggested that they should have gone to a museum. He was suspicious though, she could tell that. Sometimes she thought he could see right through her. They would have to be careful for he wouldn't approve of them stalking criminals around the town.

He came up to her and frowned. Then he put a hand on her brow, pushing her hair back a little from the temple.

'You've got a cut there. How did you do that?'

'I tripped and kind of fell against a railing.'

'You're always in such a rush, Elfie. You should learn to take your time. You're twelve now, getting to be a young lady. Perhaps you should start walking like one.'

Elfie caught Joe's grin. She'd have stuck her tongue out at him if Pa hadn't been there.

Florrie saved them from further interrogation by appearing in the doorway. 'We're running short of glasses.'

Joe turned the tap on.

'I'll leave you to it,' said Pa.

He and Florrie departed. Joe washed the glasses while Elfie dried.

'I'm sure it's where I saw him. That man. At the docks.' Elfie kept her voice down. If she closed the door that would make Pa even more suspicious. 'He's a docker.'

'But you can't have seen him for more than a year.'

'I know, but I remember him. He worked at the West India Dock. He was a gaffer. The kids all knew him. Said he was into all sorts of stuff.'

'Such as?'

'Ivory. Emeralds. Anything going.' Elfie shrugged. 'Dockers nick from ships all the time while they're unloading. Small stuff usually that they can put in their pockets. There was a couple that used to sleep under the bridges beside us. It was brandy and Jamaica rum that they nicked. They drank it themselves. They were caught one day coming out. Got a month's hard labour. Never saw them again.'

'Did you know our man's name?'

'Everybody called him Clinker. Sometimes Crazy Clinker. He had a terrible temper when anyone crossed him.'

'Sounds a nasty piece of work.'

'Oh, he is. Hey, I wonder if Dowdy would have

heard of him?' Elfie thought for a moment. 'No, I don't suppose he would. The river police are different.'

'They're armed, aren't they?'

'You should see them, with their muskets and pistols and swords! They say there's a hundred of them on the West Dock alone. Wet Bobs, they call them. They're up and down the river all the time in their row boats. Though they've got some steam launches too.'

Joe wondered how the dockers managed to get away with anything with so many police around.

'There's a big wooden fence that runs round the edge of the docks. It's as high as this ceiling. But you can break through it easily.'

'You've spent quite a bit of time down at the river, haven't you?'

Elfie admitted that she had. In some ways she still missed it, watching the big liners gliding by and the merchants' ships coming in to dock from countries all over the world: Africa, India, China, Canada, Ceylon. Bringing in ivories and spices, furs and precious stones, oils, wines, spirits, tea. There had always been so much going on, what with the loading and unloading of the cargo and the shouts of the gaffers and the police on the move and whistles blowing and then sometimes there'd be a chase on the river itself with the Wet Bobs in pursuit of a suspicious craft.

'So Clinker would have been into bigger stuff?' asked Joe.

'Oh yes. He didn't do the nicking himself of course,

not him! He'd get some of the men to bring it out and pay them a few coppers for their trouble.'

'So he was a fence. He never got caught?'

'Too smart.'

Florrie was back. Her earrings were going mad. 'Hurry up, you two! The customers are thirsty.'

They concentrated on the washing up and in her haste Elfie dropped a glass. It split into two halves on the stone floor.

'Ma'll kill me!'

'Wrap it in a bit of old newspaper and stick it in the outside bucket,' said Joe. 'And don't forget to put the lid back on.'

Elfie slunk out into the back yard and did what he'd advised. She took a deep breath of night air and looked up at the sky, catching the faint wink of a star.

'Elfie,' hissed Joe. 'Get back in here!'

She returned to the scullery and helped him carry the glasses back to the bar. The customers had moved on to another song.

'*There's an old mill by the stream*
'*Nellie Dean!*
'*Where we used to sit and dream,*
'*Nellie Dean!*

❦

They had to wait to continue their conversation until they were walking back from church the next morning. It was raining and they were sharing Joe's large black umbrella, which shielded them from Ivy and Mabel, who were walking close behind. Ivy was forever asking Elfie what she and Joe talked about all the time, only to get the same response, 'None of your business!'

'We can't just go down to the docks and look for the man,' objected Joe. That had been Elfie's suggestion. 'What could we do if we found him? We can't walk up to him and ask if he knows a lawyer called Mr Reginald Basildon-Blunt.'

Elfie could see that.

'So let us say that Clinker steals some goods at the docks, hands them on to Blunt-Face, who passes them on to the man at the station. Like a chain. This is all supposition, of course. Guess work,' he added for Elfie's benefit.

She was thinking that you'd know Joe had been schooled by Pa Bigsby. Pa was convinced he would make an excellent lawyer. So was she. She wasn't sure though how brilliant her father was at the job when he had so much money trouble. It was a good thing he'd taken Joe on. It looked as if he would need him.

'It'd be good to know what they're dealing in,' said Joe.

'Could you not have a look in Blunt-Face's office when he goes out to meet a client? He and Papa have to go out to the courts, don't they?

'I doubt he'd keep the stash in his office. Besides, Parker is always around, watching. And what do you think your father would say if he caught me snooping?'

Elfie realised that snooping wouldn't come easily to Joe. She'd had more practice.

He concluded that there was nothing much more they could do until the following Saturday. They could try going back to the shop then to see if the men met up again and if they did they might follow Clinker. Meanwhile, he would keep his eyes and ears open in the chambers to see if he could find any clues as to what Mr Basildon-Blunt might be up to.

The long black Renault motor car was standing outside the *Pig and Whistle*. Alfred Trelawney was ready and waiting for Elfie. He exchanged some words with Pa Bigsby first of all, then he let Billy crank up the engine, and they were on their way.

❦

There was another row about money in the Hampstead house that Sunday afternoon.

Mrs Trelawney greeted Elfie with the usual kiss and said how nice it was to see her. Lunch went smoothly. Afterwards Elfie read to Rosalind up in her bedroom from *The Story of the Treasure-Seekers* by E. Nesbit. The house was quiet. Rosalind had said that Mama would be having a rest. She had not been feeling too well this last week.

Mrs Trelawney came to the drawing room for afternoon tea, however. Ethel poured the tea and left them.

It was then that Mrs Trelawney said, 'Alfred, I saw

a wonderful fur coat in Marshall and Snelgrove's in Oxford Street on Friday. It fitted me perfectly and it is not overly expensive.'

Her husband put his cup down into its saucer. 'Clarissa,' he began. 'Can we wait to talk . . .?' He glanced at the children.

But Clarissa would not wait. It occurred to Elfie that she might be doing this deliberately while she and Rosalind were there.

'My other fur is quite old and we are due to visit the Manning-Blairs on Tuesday. She is always so smart. You cannot possibly expect me to go there looking shabby! I wouldn't wish to let you down, Alfred. After all, he carries a lot of influence with ministers in the government. You should remember that. He might be of use to you.'

'I don't think your fur is *that* shabby.'

'We obviously have different standards in that respect.' Clarissa's voice was still as sweet as honey. She had not run off up the stairs to fling herself face down on the bed this time. She smiled at her husband. 'I have had the coat laid aside in your name. I said you would call tomorrow to pay and collect it.'

'You should not have done that,' he said in a very low voice.

'You cannot really expect me to ask your permission every time I go shopping, darling, can you?' His wife spoke jokingly.

'Of course not. It's just that –' he broke off.

It was just that he could not afford to pay for the coat, thought Elfie.

'Come on, Elfie,' cried Mrs Trelawney almost gaily, 'Do have another sandwich! It's not like you to eat so little.'

'I ain't hungry,' said Elfie and was annoyed with herself. As soon as the words were out of her mouth she knew she had made a grammatical error, something she tried to avoid doing in front of her father's wife.

Chapter Ten:
Joe Resorts to a Bit of Snooping

The next morning Alfred Trelawney called Joe into his room. He was in the process of signing a letter. He seemed displeased with it, or perhaps with the fact of having had to write it. Nevertheless, he folded it in two and slid it into an envelope.

'I'd like you to deliver this for me, Joe.' He put a blob of red wax on the back and stamped his seal on it.

'Would you like me to address the envelope?' asked Joe.

'Please, if you will. You may do it here.'

Joe had his main desk in a side room and a small one in the lawyer's office that he used when taking dictation. He sat down and dipped his pen into the inkwell.

'The Furrier Department,' began Alfred Trelawney. He hesitated a moment before continuing in a firmer voice, 'Marshall and Snelgrove, Oxford Street.'

Joe penned the address and blotted it carefully.

'You know where that is?'

'I have passed the store.'

'Please give it to the departmental manager.'

'Yes, Mr Trelawney. Should I wait for a reply?'

'No, that will not be necessary.'

'Is there anything to collect?'

'Nothing.'

'Will there be a reply?'

'No. None. Go now, Joe! I want this matter sorted out quickly.'

Mr Trelawney was not aware that Joe would know what the matter was. When Elfie had been delivered back to the *Pig* that morning they had had time for a quick chat and she had told him about the row over the fur coat.

Joe took a bus part of the way and walked the rest to Oxford Street, where he sought out the furrier department in Marshall and Snelgrove. He asked to speak to the manager, who, when he came, looked suspiciously at him at first. Joe was used to such a reaction but got tired of it at times.

'I am delivering this on behalf of Mr Alfred Trelawney, solicitor, in Chancery Lane.'

He handed over the letter, which the manager immediately opened and read.

'I'm not surprised!' He tossed his head. 'That's why I wouldn't give her the coat to take away. Wait here please!'

Joe stood around uneasily amongst the furs while an elderly female assistant kept watch on him.

Five minutes later the departmental manager returned with another man. He did not explain who he was but said straightaway, 'You are Mr Trelawney's servant, I presume?'

'I am a junior clerk in his chambers.'

'Indeed? Well, you may give him this and inform him that I wish all these accounts to be settled within the week! Otherwise we shall have to take legal action, which will scarcely benefit a man in his position.'

He thrust a large bulging envelope into Joe's hand, turned and strode off.

Joe left and walked slowly all the way back to the office.

❧✤❧

He related the whole unhappy story to Elfie when she met him at the bus stop.

'The envelope was full of bills.'

'What kind of bills?'

'All sorts,' said Joe. 'Shoes, dresses, jewellery . . .'

'What did Papa say?' cried Elfie.

'He just put his face in his hands. And then when he looked up, he said, "What am I going to do?"'

'Poor Papa! What *is* he going to do?'

'He went out at lunchtime and sold his car.'

'Oh no!' Elfie knew her father loved his car. They'd still have their carriage of course though Mrs Trelawney tended to use that, to go shopping and visit friends. 'How will he get to work?'

Joe pointed out that he could get a bus from Hampstead into town.

Elfie brightened. 'Of course he could! I saw one this morning at the Heath. I noticed it cos it was yellow. A No. 81, and it was going to Oxford Street. I'm sure Papa would enjoy riding on the buses once he got used to it.'

They agreed that they must tell him to sit on the top deck. Elfie thought Mrs Trelawney wouldn't be pleased at her husband travelling by bus.

'But she'd better not open her gob when it's all her fault!'

'Maybe not *all*, Elfie.'

'It's her that buys the stuff!'

Joe reminded Elfie that it was her father who had bought the car. She was hoping he might be able to pay off his debts with the money he'd got from the sale but Joe shook his head.

'I can't understand though why he's so short of money. He has a lot of clients.'

Ivy put her nose out of the door. 'Ma wants to know if you two is goin' to stand there all night.'

'Are,' shouted Elfie but Ivy had disappeared inside.

'Something else happened today,' Joe went on. 'Parker became ill of a fever and had to go home in a cab. Blunt-Face told him not to come back until the fever had abated.'

'So Parker might just have to stay in his bed for the rest of the week! Wouldn't that be a bit of luck?'

'It would. And tomorrow morning both your father and Blunt-Face will be in court.'

'Oh, will they indeed?' Elfie's eyes gleamed. 'So you'll be on your own in the office?'

❧❦❧

Joe did not find the idea of snooping an easy one to accept. Pa Bigsby had always raised them to obey the Ten Commandments and respect other people's privacy and property. But perhaps Elfie was right that there might be times when you had to do something you wouldn't normally do. Especially when you were dealing with a crook, as she had pointed out. And Joe's instinct as well as his reason told him that Basildon-Blunt was involved in something underhand.

He waited for fifteen minutes after the two lawyers had left in case one of them had forgotten something and turned back. When the coast seemed clear he went quickly into Mr Reginald Basildon-Blunt's office. He had never actually entered it before, having gone only as far as the door to deliver letters or a message from Mr Trelawney. And when he had, Parker had always been around, lurking in the hall behind him.

The room was tidy. Nothing but a blotting pad and an inkwell lay on the polished mahogany desk, with its three deep drawers on either side. Joe perched on the edge of Basildon-Blunt's chair. He tried the top drawer on the right but found it locked. As were the two below. The lawyer might carry the keys with him.

He tried the top left and the one under that. The grandfather clock in the hall sounded the half-hour, breaking the silence. He straightened up, alert. The chime died away and it was quiet again, except for the muffled sounds coming from the street, the clop of horses' hooves, the cry of a carter. He tugged the last drawer and it opened! Basildon-Blunt must have overlooked that one.

There were no jewels or pieces of ivory that might have been stolen from the docks. That was what Elfie had been hoping he might find. Red-hot evidence. But Basildon-Blunt would not be so stupid. The drawer contained papers. Carefully Joe lifted some of them out and laid them on the desk. They were financial statements from various banks and companies, with accompanying letters. As Joe read he frowned. There seemed to be a number of discrepancies, things that did not make sense to him. He had brought with him a notebook and pencil and he made some notes.

He lifted his head. That noise had sounded like the front door opening!

Swiftly he replaced the papers and closed the drawer, then moved as softly as he could towards the side room, similar to the one where he worked off Mr Trelawney's office. Basildon-Blunt did not have a clerk of his own. He relied on Parker for almost everything.

Joe closed the door and stood behind it, holding his breath. His heart hammered.

Someone had come into the office. The footsteps

were heavy. The man cleared his throat and grunted. It could only be Basildon-Blunt. He was opening a drawer now and muttering to himself. Yes, it was definitely Blunt-Face himself. How long would he stay? Surely his business at the court could not be over already? What if it were? Joe could feel the palms of his hands sweating.

Then he heard the drawer being closed and a key turning. The footsteps started up again and gradually began to fade. When the front door was slammed shut Joe almost passed out with relief.

※❦❦❦❦❧❅

'You was lucky though, wasn't you?' said Elfie. 'All right, you were lucky!'

'Yes, I was.' Joe could smile about it now. 'It was a close shave.'

He had kept to his own room for the rest of the day, leaving it only when the telephone rang, which it did twice. The telephone was in a cupboard in the hall and all calls were normally taken by Parker. Joe had answered it gingerly. He hadn't used one before. Pa Bigsby said they had no need for one in the *Pig*. Anyone who wished to speak to them could come to the door.

'The first caller was Mrs Trelawney,' Joe told Elfie. 'She sounded in a real state.'

'They must have had a real dinger of a row, she and Papa. She wouldn't have been at all pleased to hear he'd sold his car and she wasn't getting her fur coat!'

'Not only that, but Mr Trelawney had had to dismiss Henry the butler,' Joe added, 'he said he'd been very sorry to let him go but Ethel was more than capable of opening the front door and banging the dinner gong.'

'Holy smoke! Mrs Trelawney will take to her bed for a month!'

'Your father has found Henry another job, with people called Manning-Blair.'

'Mrs T. won't like that either! Papa tells you a lot, Joe. He trusts you, doesn't he?' Pa Bigsby said that Joe was sensitive, and mature for his age. His calmness attracted people.

Joe also had the feeling that Mr Trelawney did not have anyone else to confide in. He probably wouldn't want to lose face in front of family friends.

'And the second call?' prompted Elfie.

'It was a man. The line was very crackly so it was difficult to make out his accent. He asked to speak to Mr Blunt. When I asked if it was Mr Basildon-Blunt he wanted he said, "Just put me on to Blunt!" When I asked if he would like to leave a message he told me to let him know that he would be there same as last week, same time, same place.'

'Did you get his name?'

'He said to tell him Jack Tar called.'

'That's not a proper name! It's a nickname for sailors, ain't it?'

'Isn't,' corrected Joe. 'But you're right, it is. It doesn't mean that the man is a sailor though.'

'And then?'

'He rang off.'

'It could have been the man at the station.'

'Or Clinker?' suggested Joe.

Chapter Eleven:
A Visit to Docklands

Elfie arranged to meet Joe at midday on Saturday again.

'I would like to think you will use your time more valuably on this occasion,' said Pa Bigsby.

'Yes, Pa,' replied Elfie.

He didn't know how valuably they were using their time! They were trying to save her father from ruin.

Joe had decided that they should not shadow Basildon-Blunt from the chambers but go directly to Leather Lane for two o'clock, or just before. That way there would be time for them to have a bite to eat and make a quick visit to the Victoria and Albert Museum.

Alfred Trelawney was going home by cab that afternoon and offered to give them a lift to South Kensington, where the museum was located. He had been travelling to work by bus but today he had to be home early. Mrs Trelawney's parents were coming to lunch. Elfie didn't think he sounded too happy about that. Rosalind had told her they were rich, her grandparents, very, very rich, so perhaps they were coming to hand some of their money over to their son-in-law. Joe doubted it, though Elfie remained hopeful. But even if they were to bail him out that wouldn't be the end of his problems. There would still be Blunt-Face to sort out. Joe said the man was forever trying to find fault with him, to trip him up over something. He felt the need to tread carefully when either he or Parker were around. Fortunately Parker had been too ill to come into the office all week. Elfie wished he would peg it but Joe had said it was going too far to wish that on anyone!

When they arrived at the museum Elfie's father asked the cabbie to pull up for a moment to let them off.

'Will you manage to get back to the *Pig* all right?'

'We'll be fine,' Elfie assured him.

Joe brandished his copy of the London bus timetable.

'You are always well-equipped, Joe.' Alfred Trelawney smiled at him. It was not often these days that he could be seen smiling. 'There is so much to see in there, whether it is art or science or architecture. And the exhibition halls are all so spread out that you'll probably be there for the rest of the day!'

Half an hour would be more like it, thought Elfie. Why hadn't Joe picked a smaller museum?

'See you in the morning, dear,' called her father.

They waved him off.

Entrance to the museum was free on Saturdays so

at least they didn't have to spend any of their money on tickets. But once they were inside they could see what Elfie's father had meant. They didn't know where to start. Joe said he would like to come back another time and look at the exhibits properly but for today it was a case of seeing something that they could report back on to Pa Bigsby. They wandered around and found themselves in a gallery devoted to Tapestries and Textile Fabrics. A group of people were being escorted around by a man who appeared to be their leader. He had a loud, carrying voice, which proved to be useful.

'Now here we have three very fine specimens of Flemish tapestry, dating back to 1507,' he announced.

'Cor!' said Elfie. 'That is old.'

'The preservation of their colour is remarkable,' the man went on.

'Write all that down in your notebook, Joe,' said Elfie. 'I'm sure it's the kind of thing Pa Bigsby would like to hear.'

Joe could write fast without scribbling.

The man was now saying something about the *Adoration of the Infant Saviour*. The group was gazing up at where it hung on the wall.

Joe made another note.

This hall then led into the Architectural Court.

Joe added that to his list and then they decided they would have to go. They had no time to waste.

Joe had worked out that a No. 21 bus would take them back in the direction of Holborn. First, though, they had to find the right stop. As they came upon it they saw a white bus taking off. It was a No. 21.

'Drat!' cried Elfie. 'We won't have time to get any lunch.'

But another bus arrived no more than seven minutes later. Once they got off they still had a fair distance to go to Leather Lane so they walked smartly.

'Once we see Clinker go into the leather shop,' said Joe, 'we will go back to the main road and wait at the nearest bus stop on the left-hand side of the road. Of course he might not come. The caller might have been someone else.'

'Are we not going to watch the shop?'

'No point. We didn't see anything last time, did we? And we want to avoid Blunt-Face seeing us as much as possible.'

Elfie was amazed at how Joe had thought everything out in advance whereas she usually rushed in and took it from there.

'But why wait at the bus stop?'

'My reckoning is that Clinker will return home by bus and that he will be going east. The chances are that he'll live fairly near the docks. He wouldn't be able to walk all the way to the East End from Leather Lane. It's too far.'

'My, you are clever!'

'It's only a guess. And I could be wrong. But it's worth following up.'

'Are we going to take the bus ourselves?'

'We'll let him get on, then we'll jump aboard at the last minute. Clinker wouldn't recognise you, would he?'

'I shouldn't think so. I was just one of the kids that hung around the dock. He never paid us any attention. Anyway, I look different now, don't I?'

Joe laughed. 'You do!'

Elfie had come to the *Pig and Whistle* barefooted, with her hair in a tangle and crawling with nits, and dressed in a skirt and shift full of holes. Now she was wearing a long blue velvet coat and laced-up-black leather boots and she had grown a good two inches in height. Ma Bigsby claimed it was due to her cooking.

※ↂ⅏҉

They returned to the doorway where they'd sheltered the previous Saturday and at two o'clock exactly Mr Reginald Basildon-Blunt, in his grey overcoat and bowler, turned into Leather Lane. He walked along the opposite pavement and on reaching the leather goods shop, opened the door and entered. Elfie gave a small, quiet cheer, but with so much noise going on in the street there was no way that she could be overheard.

She almost let out a shriek though when, passing their doorway, within inches of their face, went Clinker, the man himself. They had been expecting him to take the other side, like Basildon-Blunt. Joe put a hand over Elfie's mouth. Clinker had stopped only a few steps away to light a cigarette. He let out a few puffs of smoke, then crossed the street.

'Did you notice his pockets?' asked Joe.

Elfie had not. She'd been watching Clinker's face and worrying that he might turn and see them hiding in the doorway. She remembered only that he had been wearing a shabby fawn mackintosh and that it had been hanging open.

'He had stuff in his pockets,' said Joe. 'You could tell by the way they were weighted down.'

'With silver and gold maybe?'

'I don't know about that! Gold is really heavy.'

Clinker went into the leather shop. The door closed.

'So they are both in there now, just as before,' reflected Joe. 'Doing business.'

They stayed in the doorway for a few more minutes before moving to the main road to take up their stance on the corner.

'Let's move along a little way,' said Joe, 'and see if we can find another doorway.'

He studied his bus timetable but could not work out which way Clinker would go. There was no direct route.

Clinker reappeared after half an hour. His pockets no longer sagged, Joe pointed out.

'So he must have given the loot to Blunt-Face!'

'Looks like it.'

When Clinker reached the corner he started to walk, heading east, as Joe had predicted. He moved at a steady pace along High Holborn to Newgate Street, where he turned right, circling around St Paul's Cathedral, and continued on towards Cannon Street.

'How far's he going to walk?' grumped Elfie. Her boots were rubbing her heels. She wished she'd worn her scruffy old ones.

He was stopping now, and at a bus stop.

'Thank goodness!' said Elfie.

A couple of minutes later a blue bus, No. 60, pulled in. Clinker moved forward in the queue. They watched him pay for his ticket, then go up the stairs to the top deck.

'Quick!' Joe grabbed Elfie's hand and they ran, the last to board.

They went inside and took seats halfway towards the back. They would have quite a long ride. Elfie was tempted to take her boots off but thought better of it.

The further east they travelled the more miserable became the districts. People thronged the streets, poor people in poor clothes, some in rags. Amongst them was a sprinkling of Africans and West Indians. Pa said immigrants from the Colonies were usually to be found in the East End. The low brick houses, in their long rows, with their smoking chimneys and broken windows, looked as dejected and squalid as those who lived in them. Elfie knew that families of ten or more lived in one or two rooms and some had no rooms at all to sleep in. Men and women worked in sweatshops seven days a week, twelve hours a day for a pittance. Many could not find work. Elfie knew she was lucky.

'We must be getting near the docks.' Elfie was watching through the window.

'We'd better be ready when Clinker comes down the stairs.'

He appeared shortly afterwards and stood near the exit, ready to disembark. As soon as the bus pulled into a stop he jumped off. Two other men followed behind him, which gave some cover for Joe and Elfie. Clinker headed off without glancing round.

Elfie and Joe stepped round an old man and woman who were fighting over some rotten vegetables on the pavement. The woman's face was covered with scabs. She spat at the man when he pushed her aside and lifted up a potato. Joe was appalled. Stoke Newington was not a well-off borough but the poverty here left Green Lanes in the shade.

'We're too well dressed,' he murmured.

'Ain't nothing we can do about it now.'

Joe let that one pass.

They left a good strip of pavement between themselves and Clinker. Not that he seemed to be interested in them. From time to time he exchanged a nod with someone but did not stop. He had buttoned up his mackintosh and was walking with his hands in his pocket.

'If Basildon-Blunt paid him he'll have money on him and will want to get it home quickly,' said Joe.

They might not be attracting Clinker's attention but they were attracting others'. Eyes watched, some openly, others furtively, form beneath the peaks of cloth caps. Cupped hands were held out in front of them. Joe felt even more embarrassed because they couldn't afford to give much away and here he was in a thick winter coat while they were dressed in rags. He had fifteen shillings in his inside pocket, his week's wages, which he would hand over to Pa Bigsby. He was the biggest earner, apart from the takings at the bar, of course. The money everyone earned went towards the upkeep of the house, but Pa always handed each of them something back, for pocket money.

Joe rummaged in his pocket for some small coins. He gave a halfpenny to four or five children, which meant that a long train of kids formed and ran after them wheedling and pleading and finally cursing when he finally said, 'I'm sorry, no more.' Elfie had four pennies left from lunch. She gave two away.

Clinker turned into a street that was an improvement on the others. There was less filth, less litter and the windows of the houses were intact except for one or two. A woman, whom Ma would have considered respectable-looking, came by, pushing a baby in a perambulator. Elfie paused to look inside the pram hood and say, 'What a lovely baby!' and the mother gave them a smile, the first they'd seen since arriving in the East End.

The woman and her baby moved on. Joe was watching Clinker.

'He's going into a house! Looks like this is where he lives. Yes, he's got a key to the door!'

Clinker had gone inside. Joe took out his notebook and pencil and wrote down the address.

'I'd remember how to find it again,' said Elfie.

'It's not for us. I'm collecting evidence.'

'For the police?'

'I hope so. Eventually. Once we can piece everything together. *If* we can.'

But gradually a picture was beginning to form – though they were a long way from being able to prove anything, as Joe stressed to Elfie. He had learned enough already about the law to know that evidence had to be concrete. What they had on Clinker and Basildon-Blunt was not.

'It's circumstantial.'

'You're beginning to sound like Sherlock Holmes!' said Elfie.

Another man had turned into the street. As he passed he took a good look at them, especially Joe. Everyone looked at Joe! He got fed up with it at times, though he mostly ignored it. The newcomer was more shabbily dressed than Clinker. His shoes were down-at-heel, the laces were missing and the bottoms of his trousers frayed.

'A docker,' murmured Elfie. 'Not a gaffer. He's going into Clinker's house,' she added excitedly. 'He might be one of the men who nick stuff for him.'

'He might be coming to get paid?'

'Well, if Clinker's got the money . . .'

'I think we shouldn't hang about any longer.' Joe put his notebook away. 'We don't want to be here when the man comes back.'

'Would you like to go down to the docks?' Elfie fancied seeing the ships again.

'Do you know the way from here?'

'I can find it!'

And she did, zigzagging through old familiar streets. Again, they had to shake off following children. For a moment Elfie thought she'd spotted Gertie. But it was only another girl who looked like her. There were a number of them about.

As they neared the West India Dock they met a couple of men dressed in broad-cut trousers and blue reefer coats, with yachting caps on their heads. They were carrying swords. They gave them a hard look as they went by. Once they'd passed, Elfie told Joe they were the Wet Bobs. He'd never seen one before.

'They was sailors before, most of them.'

'Were,' said Joe.

'You can tell from the way they walk, with them being used to the sea. They say they've got muscles like steel. Course they're out all hours rowing their boats.'

They arrived at the twelve-foot wall running round the dock.

'Can't see much, can you?' observed Joe.

'There'll be a break in it somewhere.'

'Elfie, we are not breaking in!'

'All right!'

'We don't want to get arrested!'

'If we go round to the gate we might be able to squint through.'

There was a round red-brick guard house beside the gate with a guard standing out in front, holding a musket. He stepped forward when he saw them.

'What are you doing here?' His voice was not friendly.

'We was just wantin' to have a look at the ships,' said Elfie. 'Are there any big ones in? Liners?'

'Liner just docked from New York. And we've got a sailing ship, a beauty, from Norway, big timber load.'

For a moment Elfie felt homesick, for the docks and the river, and the excitement. There had been chases, with thieves running for their lives, or men overboard. Or a lighter, one of the big open boats that helped load and unload cargo, might be on fire and the bell would be clanging and the Wet Bobs rowing like mad. But afterwards, when night fell and the excitement was over, it would be back to the cold damp arches under the bridges.

She drifted over to the gate.

'You can't go inside!' the guard barked.

She came back.

He frowned. 'You remind me of someone, a girl. Used to be around. Haven't seen her in a long time.' He shook his head. 'No, you can't be her. You're too different.'

'Let's go,' murmured Joe.

The guard was still looking puzzled. 'It's the eyes,' he added.

His attention was diverted by a docker coming through the gate. The man had his hands in his pockets and he was whistling, as if he hadn't a care in the world, but Elfie wasn't fooled, and nor would the guard be, either. The docker would have done better to cut out the whistling.

'Just a moment, my man.'

The guard patted the docker's pockets.

'All right, inside!' He poked the man in the back with his musket.

'He should have tried the fence,' said Elfie.

'Come on!' Joe seized her by hand and dragged her away. 'We're going to be late home again!'

It was beginning to get dark. The days closed in early in January and heavy black clouds covered the sky. They had to try to find a bus stop, and a bus going west, but they were not sure where they were. Even Elfie, who had once known the streets well, was a bit confused. They must have taken a wrong turning.

She stopped and asked the way from an old man sitting on a stool in a doorway.

He eyed them. 'Wot are the likes of you doin' here? Couldn't spare arf a crown, could ye?'

''Fraid not.'

He laughed. 'Don't give us that!'

'We ain't got no arf crowns,' retorted Elfie.

They moved on. Joe thought the river must be on their left so if they kept going he thought they should be heading in the right direction.

They turned a corner and in the dim light they saw a large band of children gathered at the end of the street. There could be twenty or thirty in all. Joe and Elfie backed off instinctively, aware they were invaders in the other kids' territory.

'They'll skin us if they get us,' gasped Elfie. They'd

have the good clothes off their backs in a flash and leave them as naked as the day they were born. She'd seen it happen.

They ran, back around the corner, passing the old man on the stool, and down the next street. The gang was coming after them with a hue and a cry and they were armed. A hail of stones reached them, making them duck. One hit Elfie on the side of her head but she'd pulled her hood up, which was lucky for her. They turned into another street. A high wall ran along the right-hand side. Joe stopped, picked Elfie up and bundled her over the wall. Then he vaulted over himself.

'Keep down and into the wall!'

They crouched close to it. The gang thundered past, their murderous cries piercing the night.

'Git them!' That was a girl's high shrill voice. It was a voice Elfie would recognise anywhere. It belonged to Gertie.

The drumming feet passed, the cries died away and an uneasy silence descended. Gradually their eyes adjusted to the light and they began to make out shapes around them. Mounds of bricks, piles of wood – they seemed to be in a builder's yard. Elfie couldn't imagine a detective like Sherlock Holmes getting himself into a situation like this.

'There must be a gate out of here,' muttered Joe.

He groped around until he found one. A firm push and it opened. The wood was old and splintered.

'Let's go!' He held out his hand to Elfie.

It was well after seven o'clock by the time they managed to stumble home through miles of strange streets and short rides on various buses, using up every penny in their pockets.

By the time they disembarked outside the *Pig and Whistle* from the number 49 they were bedraggled and exhausted and Elfie's heels were rubbed raw.

Billy, who'd been posted outside to keep watch for them, whistled and out Ma came onto the pavement. She stood with her arms akimbo and let her eyes run over them from head to toe, taking in the state of their clothes.

'Where in the name of heaven have the two of youse been?' she demanded.

'We got lost,' said Elfie.

Ma was lost for words. For a minute or two, at least.

Chapter Twelve:
A Death and a Dispute

'Our beloved queen, full of years and honour, has passed to her rest,' Pa read from the morning paper.

'So she's finally gone to her Maker.' Ma crossed herself.

'Does that mean she's dead?' asked Sam.

'It does,' replied Pa.

Vicky, who had been called after the queen by someone – Pa thought the policeman who had found her and her twin, Albert, as babies in the street might have been the one who had named them but no one was sure – began to cry.

'It's all right, Vicky.' Ma patted her hand. 'She were eighty-one and had had a long life.'

'Was,' said Elfie under her breath. No one would correct Ma out loud. Elfie thought Ma might have been too set in her ways by the time she'd met Pa so he hadn't bothered to try to change her grammar.

'And it don't mean you is going to die, Vicky,' Ma went on. 'Just cos you was called after her.'

'She reigned over us for sixty-three years,' said Pa. 'It's the end of an era. All eras end sooner or later.'

'So we ain't got no queen now?' asked Albert, who bore the name of Victoria's long-dead husband.

'We shall have a king,' Pa replied. 'He is to be known as Edward VII and, from what we know of him, he will be a different monarch to his mother.'

'Time you was getting ready for your work, Joe,' said Ma.

But Pa thought that most businesses would be closed today. 'For several days very likely. As a mark of respect. We shall have a period of national mourning.'

Elfie hoped it wouldn't be all doom and gloom in the streets. They had had enough of that in the Trelawneys' house on Sunday. That hadn't been about Queen Victoria on her deathbed but unpaid bills at Marshall and Snelgrove.

The kitchen door burst open to admit Florrie.

'Have you heard the news?' She was wearing a black scarf of some slippery-looking material that Elfie had never seen on her before.

'We have just been discussing it,' said Pa.

'Mrs Twitchett is in a right state.' Mrs Twitchett was Florrie's landlady. 'She's crying her eyes out.'

'Mrs Twitchett?' repeated Elfie. The woman had a sharp tongue, although, as Florrie herself said, her bark was worse than her bite. Still, Elfie couldn't imagine her in tears.

Florrie fingered the scarf. 'She made me wear this. She says we'll all have to wear black until the funeral's over.' Elfie was glad to see that Florrie was still wearing her long pearl earrings.

'We shall have to see,' said Pa, who possessed three lilac-coloured suits and no other.

'Could be purple,' added Florrie.

'What about lilac?' asked Pa.

'Too pale, Pa.'

'I feared so.' He was smiling.

'We ain't putting money out on no black clothes,' declared Ma. 'We ain't got it.'

The front doorbell pealed.

'Who can that be?' said Ma.

It was unusual for callers to ring the bell. The door was locked only at night.

Joe went to find out and returned with Alfred Trelawney.

'Papa!' Elfie jumped up to greet him. He looked as if he hadn't slept all night. Could he be so upset about the queen? He was wearing a black armband.

'I came to let Joe know that we shall not be opening the chambers for the rest of the week.'

'You'll be on holiday, Joe,' cried Elfie. There might not be any work for Billy and herself either, which would leave more free time for them to get on with their investigations.

'Sit down, Mr Trelawney, do,' said Ma, 'and have a cup of tea. Make room, children. Vicky and Albert and you, too, Sam, go on up to the sitting room and play.'

They ran off at once.

'And Mabel, maybe it'd be a good idea to take Cuddles out,' added Ma. 'He's getting restless, aren't you, love?' She chucked him under the chin.

There was plenty of room now for the visitor. He sat between Elfie and Joe.

'Would you care for a bite to eat?' Ma could never let anyone come into the house without pressing food on them.

'No, thank you very much, Mrs Bigsby. I am not hungry, truly. I have eaten breakfast.'

Pa asked him what he had noticed on his way here. 'Were many people on the streets?'

'A goodly number, discussing the news. Some were hanging out black banners.'

'They must have been prepared aforehand,' commented Ma.

'They had plenty of notice,' Pa reminded her. There had been daily bulletins about the queen's health.

When Elfie's father had finished his tea he asked if Elfie might come with him for a walk in the park.

'Certainly,' agreed Pa Bigsby. 'We shall be suspending lessons for the day.'

Billy let out a whoop of delight.

'Only for the day,' added Pa.

Elfie fetched her coat and took her father's arm.

As they walked up the street they saw shopkeepers draping their windows with purple and black banners. Some had pictures of Queen Victoria on display. One man was painting his railings black. A group of elderly women on a corner were weeping.

Elfie and her father did not speak until they reached the park.

Then he said, his voice almost cracking, 'Elfie, I must tell you that my wife has gone to stay with her parents and taken Rosalind with her.'

'She's not coming back?'

'I fear not.'

'Rosalind hates her grandparents' house. She says it's dark and gloomy with big ugly furniture. Some of it's got legs that look like lions' paws. And she says she's not allowed to run about or raise her voice.'

'I know.' Elfie's father sounded even more miserable.

'What are you going to do?'

'I sent Swain over with a note and got an angry one back from my father-in-law accusing me of behaving unreasonably to his daughter, depriving her of basic necessities.'

'That's terrible!'

Elfie wished she could have a few words with the man! She'd tell him a few things he didn't know about his daughter.

'I'm so sorry, Papa.'

'I know, dear. I shall just have to wait and hope that Clarissa comes to her senses.'

Elfie wondered if Clarissa had any sense in her.

Her father said he must go to the office as he had a few things to sort out. More than a few, she felt sure. She longed to tell him what they knew about his partner Mr Reginald Basildon-Blunt but Joe had said it was much too early to reveal anything at all. They had to gather more evidence first. Only then could they let her father and Pa Bigsby know what they'd been doing. If Pa Bigsby were to find out that they were tailing people around the streets and down to the docks he would put his foot down firmly.

Joe and Elfie went out after lunch. The streets were strangely quiet and the people they met talked in hushed voices.

'It's the saddest day of me life so it is,' said Sad Sid.

Elfie wondered if that could be true.

'Me sister's beside herself,' he added.

Elfie and Joe left him standing on the corner, where he could encounter people coming in two directions. They went into the park.

Joe was contemplating their next move. Elfie agreed that it would be much too difficult to keep watch on Clinker. It was hard for Joe to keep watch on anyone without being noticed.

'It'd be good if you could do a bit more snooping around the office,' said Elfie.

Joe did not argue this time. 'I just have to try and work out a way to do it. Problem is Parker and Blunt-Face are usually around all the time.'

'We've got to do something to help Papa,' cried Elfie desperately.

'I'm doing my best.'

'Never said you weren't. Sorry,' she added. 'Didn't mean to snap at you.'

'That's all right. You're worried. So am I.'

Dusk was falling as they made their way home. The street lamps were flickering into life. Standing outside the door of the *Pig and Whistle* was a small girl. Elfie frowned. It couldn't be! It was. She ran to her.

'Rosalind, how did you get here?'

'I walked. I asked the way.'

The child's coat was wet and her blond ringlets bedraggled, and she was shivering.

'Holy smoke! That's a long way.' Rosalind's grandparents also lived in Hampstead. 'You must be fagged out.'

Rosalind burst into tears and Elfie put her arms around her.

Joe joined them and looked questioningly at Elfie over the top of Rosalind's head.

'This is my sister Rosalind.'

His eyes widened. Rosalind's did too when she saw him.

'This is Joe,' said Elfie. 'Remember, I've told you about him?'

Rosalind nodded. 'Why is he so black?'

'That's just how he is. His ma and pa lived in a different country. A hot country.'

'He's got eyes like Papa's.'

'Papa's grandma came from an island called Bermuda. It's in the Caribbean, like Trinidad, where Joe comes from.'

'I've never seen that grandma.'

'No, she's dead. A long time ago. You best come inside, sweetheart. You're all shivery.' Elfie kept an arm round Rosalind's shoulder. 'Come in and meet Ma Bigsby. She's nice, is Ma, isn't she, Joe? She's got a heart of gold. That's what our Florrie always says.'

After she'd got over her astonishment, Ma Bigsby helped Rosalind out of her coat and damp shoes and sat her down by the hearth.

'You just sit yourself there beside your sister, love, and I'll make you a nice cup of hot cocoa.'

Rosalind's sobs gradually subsided. She sipped her cocoa and ate a piece of currant bread that Ma said would do her good. Ma had told Joe to keep the others out but to let Pa Bigsby know. By the time he came in Rosalind was looking around the kitchen, taking everything in. The huge pots and pans on the shelf, the row of pinafores on their hooks and the thirteen chairs set around the big long table.

'So this is your sister Rosalind, Elfie?' Pa pulled up a chair and smiled at her. 'We've heard a lot about you, so I am pleased now to have the chance to meet you.'

Rosalind did not meet his eyes. She looked at the flames in the grate. She hadn't said a word since Elfie had brought her in.

'I don't suppose your father will know you are here, will he?' Pa Bigsby asked gently.

'He'll be worried sick,' said Elfie.

'And your mother too,' added Pa Bigsby.

If it had been left to Elfie she wouldn't even have mentioned Clarissa Trelawney! She could rot or fall into the Thames as far as she was concerned.

Rosalind turned her head. Her bottom lip was trembling. 'I want to stay here, with Elfie.'

'We shall have to contact your father, Rosalind,' said Pa. 'It is only fair to him. I'm sure you must understand that?'

The problem was knowing where he would be. He could be in his chambers or his house, or if he had found out that Rosalind was missing, he might have gone looking for her.

Pa decided to send Joe out to telephone. The telephone service must still be operating. Everything could not be shut down. 'The operator should be able to supply the numbers. Can you tell me the name of your grandfather, Rosalind, and his address?'

Rosalind would only shake her head and Elfie did not even know the man's surname.

'Very well,' said Pa. 'Joe can try the lawyers' chambers and your father's house in Hampstead.'

Joe was dispatched and returned an hour later. Mr Trelawney was not in his chambers and Mr Basildon-Blunt, who had answered the call, had no idea where he would be. Ethel, at the house in Hampstead, had said the same. Joe had left a message to ask Mr Trelawney to call at the *Pig and Whistle* urgently.

'That is all we can do in the meantime,' said Pa.

Ma Bigsby had a large pot of beef and vegetable stew simmering on the stove. She gave it a stir and looked over at Rosalind.

'You best join us at the table, darlin'. We've plenty in the pot, always do have.'

The rest of the household, drawn by the smell, began to drift in and Elfie introduced Rosalind.

'Is she staying?' asked Ivy, jerking her thumb in the girl's direction.

'Elfie has just told you her name is Rosalind,' said Pa. 'Not "she", if you please.'

'That's what we calls the cat's mother,' added Ma.

A fourteenth chair was found and squeezed in beside Elfie's.

'I ain't got room for me elbows,' grumbled Ivy.

'You said that when Gertie came,' Elfie reminded her.

'Who are you goin' to bring back next?'

'I didn't *bring* Gertie!'

'It was your fault she come though.'

'That's enough, girls,' reproved Pa.

Rosalind relaxed and began to eat. She sat very close to Elfie the whole time.

They were in the middle of their meal when the doorbell announced the arrival of Alfred Trelawney. He was in an even worse state than had been the case that morning.

'Rosalind, thank goodness!' He bent over to put his arms around her. 'I've nearly been out of my mind. So has your mother.'

'I want to stay here.' Rosalind went on eating.

'But you can't, love.'

'I *want* to!'

'Perhaps we should allow Rosalind to finish her meal?' suggested Pa.

Her father nodded and straightened up.

As Ma was starting to dish out the pudding, which was golden syrup sponge with custard, Florrie came in from the bar.

'There's a man out there wanting to see you, Pa.' Her earrings were dancing. 'Dead rude, he was. He told me to call you immediately. The cheek of him! I said to him to wait and I'd see if you were free.'

Elfie grinned. Good for Florrie! She didn't take any nonsense from anyone.

'One of those real haughty types,' said Florrie. 'You know, la-de-dah!'

But before she could say any more she was pushed aside and the man in question entered the room. He had wide waxed moustaches and they were quivering with anger.

'I am looking for my granddaughter,' he announced.

Rosalind began to cry. Her father put a hand on her shoulder and turned to face his father-in-law.

'She is *my* daughter.'

'And a fine father you are!' The man was gazing at

Rosalind as if he could not believe his eyes. 'What are you doing there, child? Sitting in the kitchen of a public house with *these* people . . .?' He was spluttering so much that he could not go on.

Pa Bigsby took over. He rose, looking very dignified in his lilac suit, and said, 'I am afraid I must ask you to leave, sir, for I do not believe we have been introduced. You have come in here as an intruder. This is a private household. The bar is public, should you wish to partake of a libation.'

Rosalind's grandfather seemed to be unable to believe his ears. His cheeks, which had previously been ruddy, turned florid. Elfie wanted to cheer but dared not. No one was uttering a sound, not even Cuddles. He had stuck his thumb in his mouth.

The intruder recovered his voice. 'I am not leaving here without my granddaughter and that is final.'

'In that case,' returned Pa Bigsby, 'I shall have no option but to call the police.'

'How dare you!'

'I do dare.' Pa never got worked up, which amazed Elfie. 'Florrie, please ask someone to fetch Constable O'Dowd.'

'I would advise you to go, Mr Clarendon-Smythe.' Alfred Trelawney spoke firmly but calmly to his father-in-law. 'It would save you a lot of trouble and this is not good for Rosalind. I am her legal guardian and she will stay with me in my house.'

'You cannot deprive her of her mother. Your behaviour

is absolutely preposterous. You will not get away with this, Trelawney!'

Rosalind spoke up then, also in a surprisingly calm voice. 'Tell Mama to come back please, Grandfather. Tell her it doesn't matter if Papa cannot afford to buy her a new fur coat.'

There was silence. All eyes were on the grandfather. He opened his mouth like a fish gasping for air and closed it again. Then he left.

'Papa,' said Rosalind, 'could we not both stay here with Elfie, at the *Pig*?'

Chapter Thirteen:
An Accusation and a Dismissal

Rosalind was allowed to spend the night at the *Pig and Whistle* on condition that she went home with her father the next day.

'You promise?' asked Pa Bigsby.

Rosalind nodded.

She was to share the mattress in the alcove off the landing with Elfie, who had taken to sleeping there full-time. That was another complaint Ivy had against her.

'How is it she always gets to do wot she wants?' she asked Ma.

'I do not!' Elfie was indignant. If only it were true!

Ma did not bother to answer. She was too busy.

In the morning, Rosalind said wistfully, 'I wish I could stay just one more night.'

'Papa wouldn't agree. And remember you promised!'

Elfie was thinking, too, that he must be lonely all on his own in the big house. The servants would be there of course but he didn't eat with them or sit with them.

He came after breakfast to collect his younger daughter but she backed away from him.

'Don't want to go!'

'You must, love. I want you to come home!'

'You can come back and visit us another time, Rosalind,' put in Pa Bigsby.

Ma gave her a cuddle and told her she'd make the syrup sponge pudding for her the next time she came, seeing as she had enjoyed it so much.

Rosalind lingered still in the kitchen.

'We have to go now, dear.' Her father took her by the hand. 'Swain is waiting.' The coachman had brought him in the carriage.

'Can Elfie not come too?'

'She's got her lessons to do,' said Ma. 'Pa Bigsby's very partic'lar about that, ain't you, Pa?'

'Very particular,' he agreed.

'I could do my lessons here. Please, Papa?' pleaded Rosalind.

'You have your own school, dear.'

'I hate it!'

'No, you don't. Now listen, you will see Elfie on Sunday. It's only two or three days away.'

'That's not long,' said Elfie. If the truth be told, she didn't think she could cope with another night in the alcove with Rosalind. The child had been restless and spent half the night kicking her in the shins.

'Oh, all right!' Rosalind scowled and gave in.

Elfie accompanied them out on to the pavement. Swain had draped the carriage in black and pinned black rosettes to the horses' halters.

Elfie gave her father a hug and a kiss and said she would see him on Sunday.

Rosalind would not wave goodbye. She was still sulking.

Mrs Trelawney returned home unexpectedly on the following Saturday. Elfie's father told her on Sunday when they were in the carriage going back to Hampstead. His wife had arrived in a cab late the previous afternoon, out of the blue, as it were, and unannounced. Elfie supposed she should feel pleased but she had been hoping they might have Sunday together, just the three of them, Rosalind, Papa and herself.

'But why did she change her mind, Papa?'

'I think she feels she acted hastily.'

She certainly had. She'd bolted!

'You know, love,' Elfie's father went on, 'I believe she really does care for me. And Rosalind, too, of course.'

'But what did her pa have to say?'

'He told her he would cut her off if she came back to me. He has an extremely low opinion of me, I fear.'

'Pa Bigsby's got a low opinion of him! But what do you mean, cut her off? Not see her?'

'Yes, that. He would also cancel her allowance and cut her out of his will.'

'Completely?'

'Yes. She'd get nothing.'

That was a blooming nuisance, thought Elfie. Not having to see the Clarendon-Smythes would be a good thing, but not the bit about the money. There were all those bills to pay.

'And will he do it?'

'I fear so.'

'Why do they hate you so much, Papa?'

'They were never keen on us marrying.'

'Why not? You're a lawyer!'

'Clarissa's parents wanted someone grander for their daughter. Preferably with a title.'

'What kind of title?'

'A lord maybe. Or at least a Right Honourable.'

'You're honourable, Papa.'

He touched her hand. 'Thank you, dear. And then, when Clarissa went home for those few days, she told them about my grandmother being a native of Bermuda. You know that some people are not open-minded about such things? They do not like people of mixed blood.'

So that must have put the tin lid on it well and truly! Elfie wondered why her father had wanted to marry Clarissa in the first place. Her head was buzzing with questions. She was forever wondering about things and never getting any answers. Ma Bigsby said when it came to love there were no answers. Look at her and Pa Bigsby! As different as chalk and cheese. Even

Florrie and Dowdy. She was all sparkly and seldom still and he moved more slowly but surely.

'Clarissa's father told her it was a mercy Rosalind had been blessed with her looks, not mine.'

'What a nerve!' Elfie gave her father a bear hug, half throttling him. 'Don't you pay them any mind! At the *Pig* we all thought he was a nasty old goat.'

Her father gave her a weak smile. 'Clarissa is unhappy, though. Well, of course she is! Anyone would be, when they're cut off by their parents.'

'Depends on what they're like.'

'I know, but it was a big step for her to take. It was brave of her to marry me in the first place.'

'Brave?' In Elfie's opinion, Clarissa had been more than lucky to get a man like her father for a husband.

'Yes, she was. To go against her parents' wishes. She lost some of her friends too.'

'Some friends!' thought Elfie. They wouldn't be worth having.

But her father was in a right basketful of trouble one way or another. She and Joe would have to get a move on and try to help him.

❧❦❧

There was little opportunity during the week. The city seemed to be drowned in mourning and on the Saturday, February the second, the state funeral was to take place in Windsor. All shops and businesses were closed. Even the train services had been cut down, to Billy's annoyance. The *Pig and Whistle* opened in the evening but they kept the noise level down so as not to upset the neighbours. Since most of them were in there anyway Elfie didn't see that it mattered.

On Monday, life in the city returned more or less to normal. Their new king Edward VII had decreed that court mourning was to last for three months, but Pa Bigsby said that did not apply to the common people, most of whom discarded their black armbands straightaway and took down their banners.

Elfie was glad. The streets in January needed cheering up. All those black and purple hangings hadn't helped, especially when the skies were grey. She liked bright colours. That was one of the reasons she was so fond of the buses. The other was that she liked being on the move. One day she and Joe might try out the new railway that ran underneath the ground, though neither of them much fancied going so deep down into the earth. Would you be able to breathe? Pa Bigsby said he presumed so as many passengers surfaced afterwards but he had no desire to be one of them. He preferred to do his travelling in the open air.

Joe went to work as usual with Alfred Trelawney that morning and returned to Stoke Newington by bus at lunchtime.

He came walking into the kitchen where they were all seated at the table. Mabel had just served the soup. They gaped at him.

'What's the matter with you, Joe, home at this time of the day?' cried Ma. 'Are you sick, lad?'

He looked unwell.

Pa Bigsby pushed back his chair and stood up. 'Something is wrong, isn't it, Joe?'

Joe nodded.

'What is it?' Elfie sprang to her feet.

'I've been dismissed.'

'Dismissed?' Pa frowned.

'Yes.' Joe's voice was wooden.

'But you can't be!' cried Elfie.

'Who dismissed you?' asked Pa.

'Mr Basildon-Blunt.'

'He can't do that!' Elfie was outraged. 'Papa wouldn't let him.'

'He couldn't stop him.'

'I'll kill that man!'

'Elfie,' said Pa softly.

Cuddles began to cry.

'I think we'd better go into my study, Joe,' said Pa. 'Come along, son. You'd better come too, Elfie.'

Elfie had no intention of being left behind. She followed hard on their heels.

They went into Pa Bigsby's study and he closed the door.

'Sit down, Joe.' Pa took him by the arm and directed

him into a seat, then he pulled up a chair for himself, as did Elfie. 'Now tell us exactly what happened.'

'They found twenty pounds in my overcoat pocket.'

'Twenty pounds,' echoed Elfie.

'But I didn't take it, Pa. I didn't!'

'It's all right, I believe you, Joe.'

'Joe'd never steal, Pa!'

'I know that, Elfie. We all do. But try not to interrupt for a moment until we hear Joe's story.' Pa turned back to him. 'Can you begin at the beginning, Joe, and tell us step by step what took place.'

'I hung my coat up on a peg in the hall as usual when I came in.'

'The coats are kept at the back of the hall,' put in Elfie.

'Elfie!' reprimanded Pa.

'Sorry. Didn't mean to.'

'As I said, I hung up my coat,' Joe continued, 'and went into Mr Trelawney's office to start work. About an hour later Parker came in and said that Mr Basildon-Blunt wanted me to take some letters to the post. So I went to his room and collected them. And while I was in there I noticed a stack of pound notes lying on a shelf at the side. I thought it a bit odd, so many bank notes sitting there in the open.'

'Go on!' urged Pa.

'I took the letters to the post office.'

'Were you wearing your coat when you went out?'

'Yes.'

'Did you put your hands in your pocket?'

Joe frowned.

'Try to remember.'

'Yes, I did. It was cold. I didn't have my gloves on.'

He never did wear gloves, thought Elfie, even though Ma always made him take them with him.

'Was there anything in the pockets?' asked Pa.

Joe shook his head. 'Nothing.'

'So you returned to the chambers, Joe?' Pa prompted.

'I hung my coat up again and went back to Mr Trelawney's office.'

'And then?'

'Ten minutes later Mr Basildon-Blunt came storming in carrying my coat. He said he'd just noticed that his money was missing and had asked Parker to search around. Parker looked in my coat pocket and there it was.'

'It was a plant,' cried Elfie. 'Joe was set up.'

'I fear you could be right,' agreed Pa.

'Parker's a right sneak!'

'So who do you think put the money there, Joe? And why?'

'Blunt-Face,' Elfie answered for him. 'Basildon-Blunt. That's who. It's obvious. He wants Joe out of there, Pa, because he's up to no good.'

'In what way?'

'We're sure he's a crook.'

'That's a big allegation to make. What evidence do you base it on?'

'That's the trouble, not much at the moment.'

Pa frowned. 'How do you mean "at the moment"?'

Elfie shrugged. Joe had given her a warning glance.

'Proceed then, Joe,' said Pa.

'Mr Basildon-Blunt called Parker to come in and back up his story, which he did, and then he threatened to telephone the police.'

'They could send Joe to prison,' cried Elfie.

At that point they were interrupted by Ma. 'Mr Trelawney's here to see you, Algernon.' She ushered him in.

Elfie ran to her father. 'You can't let them do this to Joe, Papa!'

'I feel terrible.' Alfred Trelawney collapsed into a chair and put his head in his hands. 'I know Joe wouldn't steal. But the money was in his pocket and both Basildon-Blunt and Parker were ready to swear on it in court. Basildon-Blunt gave me an ultimatum. He said that either I dismissed Joe or he would call the police and press charges. I had no choice.'

Elfie could see that. Blunt-Face was a slippery character if ever she'd seen one. And she'd seen plenty. She and Joe were going to have their work cut out to get enough to pin on him. But they must! Somehow or other.

'What is more, Mr Bigsby,' her father went on, 'I think he wishes to be rid of me too.'

'But you are partners, are you not? He cannot dismiss you.'

'No, he cannot do that. May I be frank with you, Mr Bigsby?'

'Certainly you may. I will respect your confidence, Mr Trelawney, you may be sure of that.'

Elfie's father leant forward. She sensed what he was about to say and felt sorry for him, for he wouldn't want Pa Bigsby to think ill of him. 'I have been very foolish. I have allowed myself to get into debt.'

'It's all Mrs Trelawney's fault.' Elfie could not keep quiet. 'She's bought up half the shop at Marshall and Snelgrove's.'

'Hush, Elfie,' said Pa.

'It is my fault too,' said her father, 'for allowing it to happen. For living above my means. I wished to give my wife the best. But then I made the mistake of borrowing from Basildon-Blunt.'

'I wonder where he gets all his money from,' said Elfie knowingly.

Joe gave her another warning look.

'And now, Mr Trelawney, you are unable to repay the debt? Am I right?'

'Unfortunately, yes, Mr Bigsby. What is worse, I put up my house as warranty.'

'Ah.' Pa put the tips of his fingers together and pursed his lips. 'And now he wishes to call the debt in, am I right?'

'I am afraid you are.'

'What does it mean?' cried Elfie. 'Warranty?'

Pa Bigsby answered. 'It means that Mr Basildon-

Blunt may lay claim to your father's house in order to retrieve his money.'

'And will,' added Alfred Trelawney. 'It is only a matter of time. And then I shall have lost everything.'

Chapter Fourteen: The Next Step

After her father left Elfie and Joe went to the park to discuss what to do next. There was never any privacy to be had in the *Pig and Whistle* and Ivy was all ears at the moment, sensing that something was afoot, apart from Joe's dismissal.

'What was up with your father when he come?' she had asked Elfie.

'Nothing.'

'Seemed to me he were in a state.'

'He was just in a hurry.'

Ivy had smirked. She hadn't believed her.

But Elfie had more things to bother about than Ivy.

The park was empty except for a few children playing tig.

'Joe, what are we going to do?' said Elfie urgently. 'Papa might lose his business and his house to that horrible man!'

'We need to think.'

'I've been thinking so much my head's spinning like a top.'

'We have to consider our options. We don't have many.'

Elfie groaned. 'You always spend ages considering!'

'And you're too impatient.'

She glared at him. 'I am not! You're just slow.'

He turned and looked her in the face. 'Let's not quarrel, Elfie.'

She collapsed at once. Of course she didn't want to quarrel with Joe! 'Sorry,' she muttered.

'That's OK.' He gave her a grin.

'What about talking to Dowdy?'

'He wouldn't be able to do anything. All we've got are suspicions at the moment. Nothing the police could act on.'

'You've got your notes.'

'They wouldn't be counted as reliable evidence.'

They circled the park and then went around again. The children had gone, and so had the park keeper. It had started to drizzle but neither Elfie nor Joe were aware of that. They were walking with their heads down and Elfie was doing her best to hold her tongue, hoping that Joe would come up with something.

'What day of the week was it you saw Blunt-Face meeting his contact at King's Cross? I seem to think it was a Wednesday?'

'It was.' Elfie nodded.

'I've noticed that he leaves the chambers every Wednesday around the same time.'

'The man he was meeting came in on a train at just after half past three. I remember. I looked at the station clock.'

'That was clever of you!'

It wasn't really. She'd just happened to look up. But it was nice to be called clever by Joe.

'So one thing we need to do,' said Joe, 'is to establish that this is a regular meeting.'

'We could go there on Wednesday.'

'I think *you* could. I'd wait outside.'

Elfie nodded. It was a nuisance standing out in a crowd when you were trying to trail someone. But there was nothing that could be done about it.

❧❀❧

Elfie put on an old coat and carried a shawl in her bag so that Ma wouldn't see it and ask her what she wanted with it. It was unlike Elfie to wear shawls. No comment was passed on the coat as she and Billy were going out on a delivery round.

'Joe and I have important business on hand,' she told Billy, 'so we'll need to be quick.'

Joe had already set off downtown.

Billy didn't ask any questions. He wasn't a curious boy, except where trains were concerned. They left the moment they were released after lunch. They did several deliveries at top speed, for the butcher, the grocer and the ironmonger. They trundled the goods in barrows to the customers' houses and as soon as they had finished their run Billy started to look for a carter who would oblige them with a lift.

They were not as lucky as usual today. Only two carts came by and one had a load that was so huge there was no chance of perching on top of it. The other carter passed without a wave.

'What time is it?' Elfie was hopping about, unable to keep still.

Neither of them had a watch and there was no clock in sight. They didn't want to have to walk back to the High Street.

An elderly-looking, well-dressed man wearing a bowler hat was coming their way. He looked as if he might own a watch.

Elfie approached him. 'Excuse me, sir, would you happen to have the time on you?'

'I would, young lady.' He took a watch from his pocket, flipped the case open and told them that it was exactly ten minutes past three.

'Thank you, sir.'

'Pleasure.' He tipped his bowler at her.

Ten to three! If they didn't get a lift soon she'd be too late. She wished she'd agreed to go on the bus when Joe had offered her the fare. She'd said she and Billy always got lifts. But not today.

'Here comes Tommy!' Billy waved both arms in the air.

The carter pulled up.

'King's Cross is it, lad? As if I didn't know. Get on then, the two of you!'

They scrambled on top of the wood. Would they make it in time? Elfie was not sure. The cart was slow, much slower than the bus, and the traffic was thick. When they were still about half a mile from their destination they came to a dead halt. A cart had lost its load of beer barrels. They were strewn all over the road, rolling around, causing chaos. Horns were honking, drivers shouting. Elfie and Billy jumped down.

'We'll walk, Tommy.' Elfie called up to him.

'Lucky you can. I'll be sittin' here for long enough, by the looks of it.'

'Ta, Tommy.' Billy raised his thumb.

They ran, dodging beer barrels and dawdling pedestrians, babies' perambulators and a man on a penny farthing.

The clock was striking half past three as they reached King's Cross. They were both short of breath by that time and Elfie had a stitch in her side. She had to stop for a moment to recover. There was no sign of Joe.

'See you back at the *Pig*!' Billy was off.

Elfie draped the shawl round her head and walked into the station, resisting the urge to carry on running. She saw Basildon-Blunt straightaway. He was waiting in the same place as before and he was holding a bag at his side. A stream of people were coming through the barrier and Blunt-Face had spotted his man. He turned and came walking back out towards the exit. The man followed, keeping a few paces behind, as did Elfie. Glancing round she caught a glimpse of Joe's black face in the distance.

The men went to the same café, the *Euston Cocoa Rooms*, and sat at the same table at the back. Elfie then, according to plan, retraced her steps to meet up with Joe at the side of the station. He'd been moved on twice by bobbies for loitering so he thought they'd better go inside.

'Basildon-Blunt won't come back and his mate doesn't know either of us.'

They positioned themselves a little distance away from the barrier. Joe thought that after the man had reappeared and boarded his train, Elfie should go up to the barrier and find out its destination.

'It might come in useful to know. We have to pick up any clues we can.'

Elfie liked the idea of picking up clues but wished more of them were lying around. If only they could break into Blunt-Face's house when he was at work! When she'd suggested that to Joe as a joke – well, almost a joke – he had retaliated very firmly.

'Definitely not! We don't want to end up in prison.'

He'd come near enough to it when he'd been accused of stealing the twenty pounds. Whenever Elfie thought of that she could feel her blood boil. Pa Bigsby said it was impossible for blood to boil but there were times when she could swear that hers was doing just that.

They had only half an hour to wait. Once they sighted their quarry Joe moved away and lost himself in the crowd.

The man swerved to avoid a clump of passengers and passed close to Elfie. He had with him the bag that Blunt-Face had been carrying earlier. She saw his face more clearly now. He had a birthmark on his left cheek that she hadn't noticed before and a small straggly goatee beard that reminded her of the school inspector's. Joe had said it would help to get a good description.

The man saw her clearly too. He paused for a second and frowned as if she looked familiar but he couldn't think from where. At least she hoped he could not think from where. She could have kicked herself for not being more careful. She pulled the shawl further over her face though it was a bit late now. The man walked on but before going through the barrier he glanced round. She turned away.

Ten minutes later the whistle blew and his train chugged out of the station. Elfie quickly went to the barrier and read the board. The final destination was York, though there were stops listed in between.

She found Joe waiting for her near the entrance. Some people, she noticed, were skirting around him as if they didn't want to go too close. She glared at one woman, who was wearing one of those hats with the birds' nests on top. It wobbled as she walked.

'He doesn't bite, you know,' she said, but the woman hadn't heard.

'Everything all right?' asked Joe. He hadn't heard either, which was probably just as well.

Elfie nodded.

They went outside and found a low wall to sit on while Joe took out his notebook and recorded the times of the trains Basildon-Blunt's associate had come in and gone out on. Elfie liked the word 'associate'. It was a new one to her. She also gave Joe a full description of the man.

'If we told all this to the police they could come here next Wednesday and catch them with the loot.' Whatever the loot was.

Joe was dubious. He still didn't think the police would take them seriously and Elfie suspected he was right. She'd had enough dealings with them to know that they wouldn't listen to the likes of them. To Pa Bigsby, yes. Anyone would listen to Pa.

Joe decided they should go back to Leather Lane on Saturday afternoon.

'Then we can see if Blunt-Face and Clinker meet as before. At least then we can confirm that pattern.'

Elfie was struck again by the way Joe talked. He really would make a great lawyer. If he were ever to get the chance! He wouldn't if Blunt-Face had anything to do with it. And then there was her poor father who didn't know where to turn. He might soon be out of a job himself. And homeless.

'Everything's in a mess!' she wailed. She had never felt more helpless.

Elfie went into town on Saturday ahead of Joe and called in on her father in Chancery Lane.

'He hasn't got hold of your house yet?' She jerked her head in the direction of Basildon-Blunt's office.

'Not yet.' Her father sounded despondent. 'I'm doing everything I can to raise some money. I've talked to Clarissa's brother.'

'Does she know?'

'No, I haven't told her. I dread it but I'll have to do it sometime. For even if I can raise money we will have to move to a smaller house.'

Clarissa would need her smelling salts for sure when she heard this. She kept them by her bed, so Rosalind had told Elfie. Ladies often needed them, said Rosalind, to calm their nerves and stop them fainting. They didn't have any in the *Pig*. Neither Ma Bigsby nor Florrie had ever shown any signs of fainting, even on a Saturday night when you could hardly breathe for the fug and the heat.

'So do you think Mrs Trelawney's brother might give you something?'

'He wouldn't *give* me money. It would be a loan.'

And another debt, thought Elfie. He'd never be out of the bit.

'Something might turn up, Papa.'

He smiled. 'Mr Micawber. You've been reading *David Copperfield*.'

'Pa Bigsby has got Joe reading it to us in the mornings. He's helping with our classes now that he's not going out to work any more.'

Alfred Trelawney's smile slipped. 'I feel so sorry about Joe.'

'It wasn't your fault. Joe knows that.'

Elfie kissed her father before she left and gave him a hug.

'I'll see you on Sunday, love,' he said. 'I should still have a house for you to come to!'

On the way out she encountered Parker in the hall, as she'd expected. He escorted her to the door.

'So your black friend turned out to be a thief?'

'Turned out nothing!' snapped Elfie. 'It wouldn't surprise me if it was you what put the money in his pocket.'

With that, she stamped off. Perhaps she shouldn't have said *that*. She might have alerted Parker to the fact that they were on to him and Blunt-Face. The words had come out before she could stop them. Parker had looked a bit startled before he'd closed the door. Perhaps even guilty? She decided not to tell Joe.

Chapter Fifteen:
Joe Makes a Discovery

Elfie met Joe at Holborn and they went to the café they'd gone to before and had some bread and soup. It was a bit greasy, the place, but better than some, and they weren't likely to bump into any lawyers there.

At exactly a quarter to two on Joe's watch they left, walked along to Leather Lane and took refuge in a doorway. A few minutes later they spied Basildon-Blunt in his grey coat and bowler making his way along the opposite side. He walked, looking to neither right nor left, as if he didn't want to be noticed. He went into the leather goods' shop.

'It does seem like it is a regular thing,' said Joe. 'Good!'

The words were just out of his mouth when a man stopped right in front of their doorway to strike a match. It was Clinker. Bending his head over the flame he lit the cigarette in his mouth. He then tossed the spent match away. It landed in their doorway. He glanced after it and stared them in the face, each in turn.

'Wotcher!' he said, letting his gaze rest on Elfie. 'Ain't I seen you afore somewhere?'

'Don't think so.'

'It's your eyes.'

Elfie cast them down. Why did people keep telling her that?

'You niver run about wi' some kids at the West India, did ye? The dock?'

Elfie shook her head. '*Me*? Never!'

'Could have sworn.' He shook his head, as if he were baffled and then turned his attention to Joe. 'Wotcha doin' wi' him?'

'He's my friend.'

Clinker snorted. 'You ever work at the dock?'

'No,' said Joe.

'Got a few of your mates down there. 'Ard workers, gotta say that fer 'em. Most, at any rate.'

Joe made no attempt to reply.

'If you're thinkin' of doin' a bit of nickin', the two of ye, ye'll not get far standin' in a doorway.'

Any fool would know that, thought Elfie.

With that bit of advice, Clinker left them and crossed the road.

'He'll know us again anyway.' Joe frowned. 'I shouldn't think he'd mention seeing us to Blunt-Face, though.'

'He'd better not!' Elfie gulped. What if Parker had repeated what she had said to him in the office?

'We'll have to be more careful from now on.'

Joe was right.

Clinker disappeared inside the leather shop.

'Let's get out of here,' said Joe.

At least now they had two pieces of information they could give to the police when they were ready.

❦

Elfie was dying to talk to her father about everything as he drove her over to Hampstead the following day but Joe had warned her not to. It would be a mistake. She knew he was right so kept her mouth closed. Her father seemed preoccupied with his own thoughts anyway.

In the afternoon his brother-in-law called and spent more than two hours closed away with him in his study.

'What are Papa and Uncle Horatio talking about in there?' Rosalind was cross because her father had promised to take them kite-flying on the Heath.

'Business, they said,' her mother answered vaguely.

She wouldn't imagine it could have anything to do with her. Elfie knew that her father hadn't broken the bad news to her yet. He was waiting to see what would come of his meeting with her brother.

On his way out Horatio Clarendon-Smythe looked in on them in the drawing room briefly, to say goodbye to his sister and niece. No, he would not stay to tea, thank you.

'Horatio, I don't think you've met my daughter, Elfie?' said Alfred Trelawney. His colour heightened as he spoke.

Horatio barely glanced in her direction. Elfie supposed he would not approve of her. She recalled an occasion some time before when Rosalind had said to her, 'You're illegitimate. That's because Papa and your mother were not married.'

Their father, who had overheard, had reproved her. 'It is not Elfie's fault. It was mine! I went to Canada and left her mother.'

'Mama says you'd never have married her anyway. She was beneath you.'

Elfie had flown at Rosalind and their father had held them apart.

'Elfie, you must pay no attention. It is simply ignorance on Rosalind's part.'

Rosalind had begun to cry. 'That's what Mama said.'

'I would have married Elfie's mother if my father had not sent me to Canada to learn about the timber business. By the time I returned to this country she had died and I was unable to find any trace of her. I did not know about Elfie before I left for, if I had, I would not have gone.'

His wife had been standing unnoticed in the doorway. 'Rosalind knows that Elfie is her half-sister. There was no need for you go into such detail, Alfred.'

'I rather think there was,' he had answered.

❦

Pa raised no objection on Monday morning when Joe said he wished to go to the main library to research some legal matters. Joe always managed to tell the truth, thought Elfie, even when he was hiding something. He was smarter, of course, than she was.

'A good idea, Joe.' Pa approved. 'It has an excellent reference section.'

'I'd like to do some research too, Pa,' said Elfie. There was no harm in trying but she wasn't surprised when Pa squashed the idea.

'You have lessons to do here, Elfie. Your long division needs some working on. And there's no use making a face as it won't help you.'

Once at her desk, she found it difficult to keep her mind on the numbers when there were so many other things buzzing around in her head like a bunch of bees. Anyway, who cared about dividing 6,895 by 246? When would you ever need to do it? Pa said you could never be certain what you would need in life so that the more you knew the better. It would depend, too, on what kind of work she would undertake when she was older. She would love to be a bus driver but they didn't employ women.

She kept thinking about her father's debt. She had managed to have a few minutes alone with him last night, enough to ask him how he had got on with Horatio.

'He's prepared to lend me a certain amount. Not enough to cover the house unfortunately. And the interest rates he intends to charge are high.' He had sounded gloomy.

'You'd think he wouldn't charge you any! Not when it's to help his own sister.'

'The more money some people have the less generous they are, Elfie.'

Then there were Parker and Blunt-Face and Clinker and the man who travelled on the train up and down from York. They wouldn't leave her alone either.

'How are you getting on, Elfie?' Pa Bigsby bent over her desk.

Her head jerked up. She had been far away.

'Not too well, it would seem,' he observed. 'Now first of all you must ask yourself how many times 246 would go into 689.'

'Once?'

'Try twice in your head.'

She did.

'Will it go?'

'Think so.'

'All right, you are going to multiply 246 by two and subtract the difference. What are you left with?'

'197?'

'Right. Now bring down the last figure, the 5, and see how many times 246 goes into that. And then remember after that to use decimal points. You see, you can do it when you try. It is a matter of concentrating.'

That's what he thought! Elfie had asked Florrie if she'd ever heard of decimal points and she hadn't. Yet that hadn't stopped her from doing anything she'd wanted to do.

Pa moved on to see how Ivy was progressing. She had finished the sum and laid down her pencil and was sitting with her arms folded, looking like the cat that had nicked the last drop of cream.

'Excellent, Ivy,' said Pa. 'Nice neat figures too. I think you should be able to get a job as a bookkeeper when you're old enough.'

Elfie went back to her jotter. Who'd want to be a bookkeeper? Whoever had invented long division had a lot to answer for.

She couldn't help wondering what Joe was up to in the library.

❧⟨✦⟩☙

Joe was studying a current directory of solicitors in England and Wales. He was running his eye down the list. B obviously would be near the top so he slowed down as he reached the end of the As. Basildon-Blunt should have come up almost straightaway but hadn't. Perhaps it would be listed under Blunt, though it should not be, as the surname was hyphenated. There was no Blunt there, either.

Odd.

Joe checked again, going down to the end of the Bs and then carrying on through the alphabet until he reached Trelawney, Alfred Jonathan. So why was Reginald Basildon-Blunt not listed? Joe sat, with his face between his hands. Then he had an idea. He got up and went over to the counter.

He asked if the assistant if they would have any back copies of the directory. 'Going back two or three years or more?'

The man said he would go and look in the stacks. He was away for a while but when he returned he was carrying a dusty pile of directories dating back to 1896. Joe thanked him and took them over to this seat. He started first with 1900, quickly discovering that there was no Basildon-Blunt there either. Nor in 1899. Nor in 1898 or 1897. But there was a Blunt in 1897, a Ronald Blunt. And his address was in York.

Joe sat and stared at the entry, feeling a tingling of excitement running up his spine. He had turned up something important, he felt sure of it.

'You see,' he said to Elfie later, after he had told her about his find, 'I suspect that our Mr Reginald Basildon-Blunt may not be legally registered to act as a solicitor.'

'He's a fraud, do you mean?'

'It's beginning to look like it.'

'You'd think Papa would have checked.'

'You would. But Blunt-Face may have forged his credentials so well that your father just accepted them.'

'Papa is very trusting.'

'Also,' added Joe, 'he may have already borrowed from Blunt-Face before they started up in business together. I think Blunt-Face may have set him up from the beginning.'

'Poor Papa.'

'So I think Basildon-Blunt's real name could be

Ronald Blunt. If it is, then the question is why did he change it?'

'And what's the answer?' cried Elfie.

'I don't *know* the answer. But my guess is that he could have been struck off.'

'What for? Doing something wrong?'

'That is what we have to try to find out.'

'But how?'

'I think the answer lies in York. And that means we may now have to enlist Pa Bigsby's help.'

Chapter Sixteen:
Pa Bigsby is Enlisted

Pa Bigsby sat at his desk with his fingertips placed together, the sign that he was thinking deeply.

He raised his head and said, 'That is quite a story.'

'Joe could be a detective,' said Elfie. 'He's brilliant at following up clues.'

'So it would seem. I had been wondering what the two of you were doing. I realised there was something going on. And some of it has been quite dangerous, I am appalled to hear.'

'Not really.' Elfie wanted to reassure him so that he wouldn't stop them going out and about in the city in future.

'Following this man called Clinker seems to me highly dangerous!'

'We was careful.'

'Were,' said Joe.

Elfie shook her head, annoyed with herself.

'You know there are parts of London I don't permit you to go into.' Pa looked serious. 'Especially after Joe was attacked by that mob last year. And especially not the docks!'

'We had to,' insisted Elfie. 'We'd no choice.'

They hadn't told Pa about the gang pelting them with stones. They had agreed there was no need to tell him every single little thing.

'You have put the evidence together very well, Joe.' Pa was studying the notes in his book.

'Thank you, Pa.'

'You have made a convincing case, I must say. It would certainly appear that this man Blunt is a fraudster and involved in some sort of criminal activity connected to the docks.'

'It'll be handling stolen stuff off the ships,' Elfie informed him. 'Goes on all the time. Clinker was known for it.'

'Your knowledge has obviously been very useful, Elfie.'

'He's trying to ruin my father, that Blunt-Face! Or whatever his name is. We've got to stop him, Pa.'

'We shall do our level best. The first thing we must endeavour to find out is what, if anything, happened in York.'

'We could go there,' Elfie suggested hopefully. 'The three of us.'

'That would be impractical. And expensive. There are ways of obtaining information without actually going to the place itself. I think we might have a word with our own Constable O'Dowd.'

'Dowdy wouldn't know anything about York. Least, I don't think he would.'

'He does not need to *know* anything, Elfie. But I can think of a way in which he might be able to assist us.'

'I told you Pa would have an idea,' said Joe.

'Get your coats on,' said Pa. 'We need to pay a visit to the police.'

Dowdy was in the station and surprised to see them.

'Not come on business, I hope?' he joked. 'Nobody's been misbehavin' at the *Pig*?'

'I am happy to say that they have not,' replied Pa. 'At least not sufficiently for me to have to call in the police,' he added, giving Elfie and Joe a sideways glance.

'Florrie all right?'

'Florrie is exceedingly well, Kieron.'

'She's just bought herself a new blouse,' put in Elfie. 'It's gorgeous. Pale lilac satin, a bit like the colour of Pa's suit. Wait till you see it! You'll love it, Dowdy.'

'I'm sure he will, Elfie.' Pa looked back at Dowdy. 'May we have a word in private, Kieron? Would that be possible?'

Dowdy looked taken aback but said he'd ask the other constable to take over for him at the desk. There didn't seem to be much going on, as far as Elfie could see. The place was dead. She'd thought police stations would be full of criminals waiting to be charged and brought to justice. Well, one or two at least.

The second constable obliged and Dowdy invited Pa Bigsby to follow him into a small back room.

'I'm afraid we are all coming,' Pa told him. 'Will there be sufficient chairs?'

'I'll fetch another.'

Dowdy left them and returned carrying a chair. He seated himself behind a table and they sat in a row on the other side facing him.

'Now what can I do for you?' he asked. He suddenly sounded very businesslike and not like the Dowdy they knew.

'We need to find some information about a lawyer with a suspicious record in the city of York,' Pa informed him.

'I've never set foot in York.'

'You see,' cried Elfie, 'I told you.'

'Hush, dear. Let me speak.'

'Sorry, Pa.'

'Would it be possible, Kieron, for you to make a telephone call to the main police station in York?'

Dowdy was looking dubious. He wasn't used to working with police stations far afield. He kept mostly to his own patch.

'I am sure the telephone operator would be of assistance in acquiring the number,' Pa went on.

'It can often take a good while to get through.'

'I appreciate that you must be very busy, Kieron. So

perhaps I could make the call? Or Joe? He has more experience with these machines. And then when he has made the connection he could hand the receiver over to me so that I would do the talking.'

'I'd need to ask the sergeant. What's it all to do with, Pa?'

Pa Bigsby gave him the basic facts about Alfred Trelawney and his partner Reginald Basildon-Blunt, whom they suspected to be Ronald Blunt, formerly of York.

Dowdy went to consult his superior and returned with him.

'Good day to you, Mr Bigsby,' said Sergeant Feather. He paid the occasional visit to the *Pig* when he was off duty.

The two men shook hands and then Pa set out the reasons for his request again. 'Fellow sounds like he's a bit of a no-gooder,' agreed the sergeant. 'I see no reason why Mr Bigsby shouldn't speak to them in York, Constable.'

'If I might say that I have your permission and that I am telephoning from this station?' asked Pa.

He was always so polite, thought Elfie. How could anyone ever refuse him anything?

'Certainly you may, Mr Bigsby. And Mrs Bigsby, is she well?'

'Very well, thank you, Sergeant.'

'Good. I'll leave you with Constable O'Dowd then.'

The sergeant departed and Dowdy took them back

to the reception area where the telephone was located on the back wall. Joe unhooked the receiver. He said the line was crackly and he could hear other voices in the background, faintly. Finally, he got the operator for the local exchange and explained his problem. She put him through to another operator who dealt with directory enquiries.

'I could hardly hear her,' he said, covering the mouthpiece with his hand.

'Was it a woman?' asked Pa.

Joe nodded.

'I believe they have just started to employ a number of women.'

Elfie wondered if she would like to be a telephone operator. Talking to people all over the country could be quite interesting, though, on the other hand, you'd be stuck inside a stuffy room all day. It was bound to be stuffy since you wouldn't be able to open the windows. If you did, you'd have the noise of the traffic in one ear.

Joe was speaking again, requesting the number in York. As he repeated it Pa wrote the digits down, using Joe's notebook.

'Splendid!'

Joe had to go through two more exchanges before he finally reached the main police station in York. As soon as he heard the ringing tone he passed the receiver over to Pa, who was already on his feet, waiting to take it.

'Ah, good afternoon. My name is Mr Algernon Bigsby and I am calling you from the police station in Stoke Newington in London.' He carried on with his tale, finishing by saying, 'I would be most grateful if you would be able to look in your records and see if you have any mention of Mr Ronald Blunt. Possibly in 1897 or 1898? Thank you very much indeed. Yes, I appreciate it may take a little time. I will give you the number of the station here.' He read it out, said thank you again and hung up the receiver.

'We may have to impinge on your hospitality a little longer, Kieron,' he said.

'No, problem, Pa. Glad to be of help.'

'Your colleague in York was most helpful.'

'How long do you think it'll take, Pa?' asked Elfie.

'Twenty minutes or two hours. Impossible to predict. But you do not have to stay, Elfie. I can see you are restless. You may run off home if you wish.'

'I ain't going anywhere.' She was indignant at the suggestion. This was their case, hers and Joe's.

'Am not going anywhere,' corrected Pa.

The station door opened and Mrs O'Grady came bursting in.

'I've been robbed!' she cried.

A bit of action at last, thought Elfie.

'Two lads, no more than nine, ten years old . . .' Mrs O'Grady was heaving for breath.

To Elfie's annoyance, Dowdy suggested the other visitors went and sat in the back room. Apart from the fact that it was cold and gloomy in there, she would miss the rest of Mrs O'Grady's story.

'You might go out and buy me an evening newspaper, Elfie?' suggested Pa. 'It will only take you a few minutes so you won't miss anything in that time, I'm sure. And we might as well catch up with the news while we wait.'

He gave her a penny. Joe said he'd stay with Pa, in case the telephone should happen to ring.

On her way out Elfie stopped at the front desk.

'I was very sorry to hear you were robbed, Mrs O'Grady. Did they get much?'

'A slab of toffee and a handful of my best striped balls. It was the cheek of them! Right in front of my nose.' She jabbed hers to make the point. 'And Constable O'Dowd says he's too busy to go out and look for them!'

'Had you ever seen them before?'

'Never.'

'Mustn't be from round here, then.'

'There was two of them. Cheeky beggars!'

Elfie left Dowdy to deal with Mrs O'Grady.

The afternoon was closing in. It was a time of day that Elfie and Joe both liked, with the street lamps and the shop windows lit and smoke puffing from the chimneys into the hazy sky. Pa said there was too much smoke puffing from chimneys. That was why they got so many fogs. Pa said that if he had enough money he'd take them all out to live in the country in the fresh air but Elfie wasn't sure she'd fancy that. Not to live all the time. There mightn't be enough going on.

And they'd miss Florrie and Dowdy and Sad Sid and Mad Meg and Frankie on the harmonium.

She didn't dilly-dally too long, in case she'd miss the news as it came in. She bought Pa's newspaper and hurried back to the station.

'Mrs O'Grady gone?'

'Just got rid of her.' Dowdy sighed. 'How does she expect me to go chasing round the streets looking for two boys with a slab of toffee and some striped balls in their pockets? Not that I approve of them doing that of course. But there's a limit to my duties. And by the time I'd catch up with them the sweets would be inside their bellies.'

The telephone shrilled from the wall.

'*Dowdy!*' shrieked Elfie.

'All right, I hear it! I'm going.'

He went to the telephone and unhooked the receiver. 'Stoke Newington Police station. Who is speaking, please?' He listened, frowning, as if he was having trouble hearing. 'Is it Mr Algernon Bigsby you wish to speak to? It is. One moment, please.'

Elfie flew along the corridor into the back room.

'It's the police from York,' she yelled.

Chapter Seventeen:
The News from York

'I wouldn't be surprised if they heard you in York,' said Pa Bigsby, as he followed Elfie along the corridor.

She wished he'd hurry up. But he was walking as he always did, at a measured pace. That was how Joe described it. She supposed she couldn't really imagine Pa running, not unless the *Pig* was on fire or if someone was attacking Ma. She could take care of herself, though. A man had come in around the back of the bar one night and tried to rob the till right in front of her nose, the way the two boys nicked Mrs O'Grady's sweets. Ma had been alone but she'd seen the man off. She told them all later how she'd picked up the brass poker and escorted him out of the door.

The telephone receiver was dangling from its cord against the wall. Elfie hoped the policeman in York would still be at the other end.

Joe lifted the receiver and put it in Pa's hand.

'This is Algernon Bigsby speaking.' He listened intently, with his head bowed. 'That *is* interesting!'

'What is it, Pa?' cried Elfie.

'Shush.' Joe put his hand over her mouth.

'Most interesting,' said Pa. 'So Mr Ronald Blunt was charged with forging a cheque and served two years in prison? From 1897 to 1899, you say? He would then be struck off the register and banned from operating thereafter as a solicitor, would he not?' Pa concentrated on listening again, cupping his free hand round his left ear. 'I am not surprised that he has not been seen since in your fair city. I have reason to believe that he is here in London practising law under an assumed name. Could I trouble you to send me a copy of those details, care of Sergeant Feather? To the Stoke Newington Police station. By express post? Yes, indeed, we shall be taking it further, fear not. Thank you very much, sir, for your time. We may well be in touch again.'

Pa hung up the receiver and turned round.

'So he is a crook then?' At last Elfie was allowed to speak.

'He most definitely is. We have to establish of course that Ronald Blunt *is* Reginald Basildon-Blunt.'

'He must be,' said Joe. 'It would be too big a coincidence, and it all fits, even that the man he meets comes from York.'

Pa nodded. 'The inspector also told me that other charges had been raised against him but were dropped due to insufficient evidence.'

'We will be able to prove he's acting illegally as a solicitor,' said Joe.

'And that would get him off Papa's back!' Elfie wished she could see the man's face when he was kicked out of her father's chambers. And Parker along with him. 'Would the police arrest him?' She turned to Dowdy.

'If he's committing fraud, he'd be charged, no question.'

'And there is something else that he is involved in,' Joe reminded them.

'The thieving from the docks,' finished Elfie. 'The three of them, Blunt-Face, Crazy Clinker and the man from York.'

'And Parker too probably,' Joe added.' I think he's in on it. In a minor way. He watches out for Blunt.'

'Like a henchman?' suggested Dowdy.

'This all requires some further thought.' Pa stroked his beard.

'We've got evidence,' Elfie reminded him.

'Only what you and Joe have observed. That would not constitute proof. Nor do we know what it is that they are handling.'

'Stolen goods of course.'

'But they would have to be found with the goods on them, Elfie.'

'Caught in the act?' said Joe.

'Exactly!' said Pa Bigsby.

'I think I'd best consult Sergeant Feather.' Dowdy was beginning to look a trifle worried. He went off scratching his head.

Elfie thought he probably hadn't had to deal with such big-time crooks before. Crime in Stoke Newington, according to Florrie, who got it from Dowdy himself, was mostly petty theft, domestic rows and drunken fights. There was seldom anything much exciting going on, although having a mad dog set on you by a thief, had been exciting enough, she supposed. Florrie had got all worked up after it had happened to Dowdy. Her earrings had gone mad. Pa had had to calm her down.

'Kieron coped with it,' he had said, 'and was none the worse for the experience. He brought the dog and its owner under control. If you are going to be a policeman's wife, Florrie, you will have to accept that your husband may sometimes find himself in difficult situations.'

Pa Bigsby always had something wise to say.

They were waiting for it now.

'The crimes are not actually being perpetrated in this district,' he mused.

'They're all over,' said Elfie. 'The docks. King's Cross. Chancery Lane. Leather Lane.' She ticked them off on her fingers.

'All right, Elfie.' Pa stopped her before she could think of anything else. 'Sergeant Feather may have to refer the case to Scotland Yard. It is probably too much for him to handle.'

Elfie had mixed feelings about that. She liked the idea of working with Scotland Yard but there might be more chance to be involved if Dowdy and Sergeant Feather were running the investigation.

'They'll need us to identify the men,' said Joe.

Pa agreed. 'But I doubt they would let you actually be there when they make the arrests.'

Elfie said nothing. They'd see about that when the time came.

Dowdy returned with Sergeant Feather, who, it seemed to Elfie, was looking rather puffed up with himself.

'Well now,' he began, 'this is a rum do. We shall have to deliberate and then decide on a course of action.'

'It is imperative that we talk to your father as soon as possible, Elfie,' said Pa Bigsby.

The sergeant offered the use of their telephone.

'That is most kind of you, sir.'

'If you speak to Mr Trelawney at his chambers, Pa, he might be overheard,' pointed out Joe.

'Oh, he would, by Parker!' Elfie did not doubt it. 'That snoop!'

Pa thought it might be best to leave a message at the house in Hampstead. Elfie had the telephone number in her head. She warned Pa that he would need to repeat the instructions twice over to Ethel. She answered the telephone now that Henry, the butler, had gone.

Pa dialled and asked the operator to put him through to the Hampstead number. 'Ah, good afternoon. My name is Mr Algernon Bigsby. Yes, Bigsby.' He spelt it out. 'B– I – G – S – B – Y.'

'Not sure if Ethel knows her alphabet,' commented Elfie.

'I wish to leave a message for Mr Trelawney. Could you ask if he would please come to the *Pig and Whistle*? Yes, the *Pig and Whistle*. Preferably this evening. The matter is urgent. Will you remember to tell him that? Thank you very much.'

❦

Alfred Trelawney arrived in a cab just before eight o'clock that evening.

'Thank goodness!' he exclaimed when he saw Elfie. 'I thought perhaps you were ill.'

'No, but we've got lots of exciting things to tell you, Papa. Wait till you hear!'

'I think we shall repair to my study.' Pa led the way.

Once they were seated, he suggested Elfie and Joe tell their story.

'It's Joe's story really,' said Elfie. 'He did most of the thinking.'

'I think you had a hand in it, though, Elfie! But perhaps Joe could start and give your father the facts and then you can fill in the parts you were involved in. I would scarcely expect you to remain silent throughout.'

He was right of course. Elfie had more than a few things to say. And from time to time Alfred Trelawney himself could not resist breaking in.

'What a fool I was to allow myself to be taken in by such a man!'

'How could you have known he was a fraud?' Pa put to him.

'I should have checked his credentials more thoroughly.' Elfie's father bowed his head. 'It was remiss of me but I was in debt to him and so I felt obliged to accept his proposition. I feel truly ashamed of myself, Mr Bigsby.'

'It's all right, Papa.' Elfie put her arm round his shoulder. 'He's not going to get away with it.'

'We all make mistakes in life,' said Pa Bigsby.

Elfie couldn't imagine what Pa's could be.

A tap on the door announced Florrie.

'Kieron's here to see you, Pa.'

'Tell him to come in, please, Florrie.'

Dowdy came in and Pa Bigsby introduced Alfred Trelawney.

'Sergeant Feather has referred the case to Scotland Yard, Pa,' said Dowdy. 'It's a bit too big for us to handle. An inspector's coming to the station first thing tomorrow morning and would like to see you all there, if that would be convenient?'

'What time did he suggest?'

'Eight-thirty.'

'We shall be there,' declared Pa Bigsby.

They arrived ten minutes early to find Sergeant Feather holding the letter from York, along with a newspaper cutting.

'This would appear to be our man.' The sergeant pointed to a photograph.

They crowded around the desk.

The photograph was sufficiently clear for both Joe and Elfie to confirm without the shadow of a doubt that Reginald Basildon-Blunt was, in actual fact, Ronald Blunt. There was a long paragraph about his misdeeds and his subsequent sentence of two years in prison.

'That's him all right!' said Joe.

Chapter Eighteen:
The Stakeout

When Elfie opened her eyes on Saturday morning she sprang straight out of bed. She was first in the bathroom. It was just beginning to turn light outside and everyone else was sleeping. She could hear Mabel snoring as she always did when she lay on her back. Pa said she could do to get her tonsils out but he considered the operation to be too much of a risk.

Elfie washed and dressed and took time to brush out all the tangles in her hair. This was going to be an important day and she didn't want to look in any way scruffy. They had an engagement with Scotland Yard.

If only the rest of them knew what they were up to! They wouldn't be sleeping, that was for sure. The only person in the house who did know, apart from Joe, Pa Bigsby and herself, was Ma, and she wasn't happy about it.

'I don't like the idea of the two of them getting

involved with a bunch of crooks, Algernon,' she'd said to Pa. 'Nor you, either, for that matter.'

'They already have had some involvement with these men, and on their own, in dangerous places. Today, the police will be thick on the ground, and all that Elfie and Joe will be required to do is identify the man they call Clinker and signal when they see him approaching. They have been instructed to stand well back and keep out of the action.'

Clinker was not known to the police, not under that name at least. Joe had given his address to the police but they had obviously not wanted to go to his house and check up on him. That would have given the game away. Under no circumstances were either Clinker or Blunt to be alarmed. The police had been impressed though by the way Joe had noted down all their details.

During the week Alfred Trelawney had gone to his chambers every day and behaved perfectly normally to Blunt and Parker. Blunt had raised the question of the loan again and said that if it were not repaid in full the following week he would move to call it in and demand that the house in Hampstead be sold.

Elfie felt as tight as a newly-wound clock spring. She left half her porridge and although Ma tutted she didn't fuss for she knew that this was no normal day. How could it be when you were going to be working with an inspector from Scotland Yard!

Joe didn't eat too much at breakfast either. He did finish his porridge but ate no bread and butter.

Ivy's eyes swivelled from Joe to Elfie. 'Wotcha up to?'

'Never you mind!' retorted Elfie. 'It's private.'

'Where you goin'? To town?'

'Maybe.'

Ivy turned to Ma. 'Can I go, Ma? You said we could go one Saturday, me and Mabel?'

'But Mabel's going to visit her aunt in hospital. You know they took her in yesterday.'

'You could go to the trains with Billy,' suggested Elfie. That was far enough away from Leather Lane.

'I'm not wantin' to go to no trains. Ma, you said we could go to a café with Joe and Elfie. Why do they always get to go? It's not fair.'

'You can go another day, love. I need you to give me a hand with Cuddles today, with Mabel being away. But don't worry, you'll get a special treat, I promise you. You and Mabel.'

'Please may I leave the table?' Elfie was already up on her feet.

'You may,' said Ma. 'But don't be running, mind.'

Elfie did run, all the way up the stairs.

They met in Pa's study, the three of them, to go over the final arrangements. Pa warned them that they were to keep well back from the action.

'You understand, Elfie?' He gave her a severe look.

'Yes, Pa.'

He did not ask Joe.

'After today Papa will be free of that horrible man!' cried Elfie.

'We hope so, anyway,' said Pa.

'They might have changed their arrangements,' said Joe.

'They've *got* to be there! For Papa's sake.'

'Your father has been too trusting, I fear, Elfie.' Pa Bigsby sighed.

'He needs Joe to look after him.'

'I think you might be right.' Pa smiled and rose from his chair. 'Let us be on your way then. We cannot afford to be late!'

⁂

They took up their positions. Elfie stood in a doorway near the top of Leather Lane while Joe was in one on the main road, near the bus stop. When Clinker came into view Joe was to give the nod to a constable standing nearby, who would be wearing everyday clothes and a cloth cap and reading a Racing Paper. The bobby would then follow a few paces behind Clinker.

Another policeman, similarly dressed, was stationed in a doorway on the opposite side of the street from Elfie. She could see him. He, too, had some kind of paper though you could tell he wasn't really reading it. He kept looking up. When she saw Clinker approaching she was to wave, that was all, and stay well back in the doorway. The bobby across the road would tail Clinker the rest of the way up the street. Other members of the police force, including the inspector from Scotland Yard, were sited at various places around the area.

First of all, they expected that Ronald Blunt, alias Reginald Basildon-Blunt, would arrive in the street and make for the leather goods' shop.

And so they waited. The bobbies might find it easy to stand still without fidgeting but Elfie did not. They were trained in this kind of business. Her spine tingled. She longed to take a quick peek along the street but resisted. She pictured Blunt leaving his house and heading up the street towards Holborn Circus. He should have reached the main road by now.

A nearby clock struck two.

What if neither of the men turned up! She and Joe would look like real idiots, leading the police astray, wasting their time. The Scotland Yard inspector wouldn't be pleased. He was an important policeman. You could tell from the braid around his hat.

When Blunt came into view on the opposite side of the street Elfie almost called out but stopped herself in time. As he had done on previous such occasions he wore a grey coat and a grey bowler, not his legal clothes. Elfie waved and the policeman nodded. Blunt looked neither to right nor left but kept his head down. He did not want to attract attention, that was as plain as the nose on your face, and he seemed to suspect nothing unusual for he did not falter. On reaching the leather goods shop he glanced round very briefly and then entered.

Elfie breathed a sigh of relief. So far, so good. It was beginning to look as if everything would go according to plan. She relaxed a little. The policeman opposite was folding up his paper.

They waited again. Elfie had never known the minutes to pass so slowly. Clinker was taking his time but then he had before, she remembered. There had been an interval each time between the arrival of the two men. Joe had pointed out that they wouldn't want to arrive hot on each other's heels.

She risked a peek, just a quick one. Clinker was coming! She pulled her head back in quickly, waved to the policeman, and shrank into the cover of the doorway, pulling her hood over her head.

As she did so, an arm grabbed her around the neck and whirled her about. She looked into the narrowed, murderous eyes of Clinker, and felt his breath, reeking of cigarette smoke, on her face. He turned her then so that she faced the street, with him behind her, holding her arms locked together into a vice-like grip.

'You little brat,' he snarled. 'What are you up to then? I've seen you and your darkie friend around once too often.'

The policeman was coming from across the street. He was running, dodging traffic, blowing a whistle, his cheeks puffed out and red.

'Settin' me up, was you?' Clinker jerked Elfie's arms and she screamed.

He yanked the hood back from her head.

'Lovely hair ye've got.' He stroked it and she trembled. 'Nice and silky. Not like wot it used to be when you was livin' under the bridges. I remember you from there.'

Then she felt something cold against the skin of her neck. Her heart banged in terror. He had a knife!

There were two policemen on the pavement in front of them now.

'Let her go!' yelled one.

'Are you jokin'?' Clinker laughed. 'And don't you dare come near! I've got a nice sharp little blade right 'ere at the side of 'er neck. It is real sharp, ain't it, dear?'

She felt the prick of it and tried to scream again but her throat seemed blocked. He could kill her! He'd killed before – she'd heard the stories.

'You can't get away!' bellowed the constable. 'You're surrounded.'

'We'll see about that.'

More policemen had arrived to form a semicircle around the doorway. Joe stood behind them. He looked terrified.

'She won't git out of 'ere alive unless you lets me go,' said Clinker. 'One little slip and her nice soft skin'll be slit.'

Chapter Nineteen:
A Stand-off

The inspector from Scotland Yard had arrived and the crowd was being moved back by the other policemen.

'Out of the way, please! Move along there now!'

Joe did not move. He stood completely still on the pavement, his large dark eyes staring out at her. Elfie wanted to shout to him but she couldn't speak. She couldn't do anything. She was petrified. Now she knew how a bird would feel in the jaws of a cat. She remembered, too, how men like Clinker worked. If anyone double-crossed him they'd end up in the dock. She'd seen them, floating, face down, in the filthy water.

'Now then,' the inspector began, addressing Clinker over the top of her head, 'you must realise that there is no chance of escape for you so I would advise you to release this child straightaway and come quietly. It'll be the worse for you if you don't.'

'So you sez. I'll take this girl all the way with me if

I has to. Anybody try to stop me and the blade goes in, ever so nice and easy like. I ain't jokin' neither.'

'He's not,' cried Elfie, finding her voice for a moment.

'How far do you think you can get?' asked the inspector. 'You're a long way from home and we know where you live. You'll have no hiding place.'

'I wouldn't say that. I've plenty places I can go. Places you'd never even dream of. Fetch us a cab, guvn'r! At the double!'

The inspector's face turned a dark shade of red and his eyes bulged with anger.

'I cannot possibly ask any cabbie to drive you,' he snapped.

'Fetch me one! Oi, you!' shouted Clinker. A cab had stopped in the street.

'Git him!' barked Clinker. 'Now!'

'I certainly will not.'

'Suit yerself.' Clinker put the tip of the blade into Elfie's neck. She screamed. The onlookers sucked in their breath.

Joe tried to push forward but was held back. Pa Bigsby was there, too, now, and Elfie's father and Dowdy. They all looked as helpless as she felt.

The inspector strode over to the cab and exchanged a few words with the cabbie, who immediately jumped down from his box and made off. The inspector called out to one of the policemen to hold the horses and then he returned, pursing his lips, to continue his conversation with Clinker.

'No cabbie will take you. I cannot force them to. Best come to your senses, my man.'

'I ain't nobody's man. Git one of your own to drive us. But warn him! Any messing about and I'll do a bit of fancy cutting.'

The inspector went off to confer with his men and when he came back he said, 'Constable O'Dowd has offered to drive.'

Maybe Dowdy would think of something! Elfie latched on to that hope. But what *could* he do when Clinker had a knife at her neck? A man who would stop at nothing.

'Move everybody right back, guv,' continued Clinker, 'and git your bobby to bring the cab close to the pavement. I want nobody nowhere near us.'

With a grim face, the inspector did as he was told. A wide passage was cleared across the pavement and roadway. All traffic had been stopped. A terrible quiet fell over the street. It was as if the Queen had died again.

Clinker prodded Elfie. 'Move now, dear. Ever so slowly like. Don't try a runner cos you ain't goin' to make it.'

She inched forward with Clinker stuck to her back like a limpet. They advanced across the pavement at snail's pace. The blade was there all the time, nudging her, warning her. They stepped down from the pavement onto the road. They were only a foot or so from the cab now. She kept her eyes fixed straight ahead. Dowdy was sitting up on the box, holding the horse's reins, his eyes full of concern. The crowd remained hushed.

The next thing happened so fast that Elfie almost did not see it. In a flicker, out of the corner of her eye, she glimpsed an arm go up and something come whizzing through the air. Clinker fell backwards, the knife dropped to the ground and she was free! The police were on top of Clinker.

Elfie ran into the outstretched arms of her father. Tears ran from his eyes, as they did from hers. Pa Bigsby and Joe were beside him. Pa Bigsby was wiping his eyes with a large white handkerchief. Joe looked too shaken up either to cry or speak.

Pa Bigsby laid a hand on his shoulder. 'Well bowled, Joe lad! I always knew it was a good idea to teach you boys cricket.'

'I thought I'd risk it. It wasn't too difficult. Clinker stood a good head above Elfie.'

'Still, it was quite a feat to get him right in the centre of the forehead. It was brave of you to try.'

''Exceedingly brave,' added Elfie's father. 'I don't know how I'll ever be able to thank you, Joe.'

Elfie knew. He could take Joe back into business with him. She'd tell him later, when they were on their own together.

The police had handcuffed Clinker and dragged him up into a sitting position. His head lolled backwards and blood ran from his forehead.

The inspector lifted a piece of paving stone from the ground and held it up. He called over to Joe. 'Good shot, son!'

'Joe is an excellent overarm bowler,' replied Pa Bigsby.

'Well, it's certainly come in useful.' The inspector turned to Elfie. 'He saved your life, young lady.'

'I know! He's my best friend.' She couldn't stop trembling. She put out her hand and Joe took it and held it fast. He had a strong, reassuring grip.

Her father had pulled out his handkerchief and was dabbing the side of her neck. When he lifted the white cloth it showed only a few drops of blood.

'I thought my heart was going to stop when you cried out!'

'We all did,' said Pa Bigsby.

'You should look in his pockets, Inspector!' Joe nodded at Clinker. 'He was carrying something. In his right pocket.'

The inspector rolled Clinker over and delved into his right pocket. He brought out a bag made of chamois leather.

'You were right, lad!'

'Open it, please!' Elfie couldn't wait to find out what was in there.

The inspector undid the drawstring fastening the neck of the bag and peered in at the contents.

'Cor love a duck!' he exclaimed, his speech slipping.

'What is it?' Elfie pressed forward with Joe.

'Precious stones, I would say.'

The inspector slipped his hand into the bag and came up with his palm full of sparkling green gems. The bystanders gasped.

'Emeralds,' Pa Bigsby spoke with awe. He took out his monocle and bent over to get a better look. 'Exceedingly fine ones, too, as far as I can judge.'

'Probably from India or some place similar,' said the inspector.

'They'll have been nicked off a ship,' Elfie informed him.

'No doubt they will have been. Our river police are agile men but some scoundrels manage to slip through the net.'

Quite a number, thought Elfie, more than they might know, though most of the dockers didn't get away with big stuff like this.

Dowdy had jumped down from the box, and the cabbie, who had been lurking up the street, returned to reclaim his vehicle. Dowdy bid him wait a moment, then he came over to Elfie. 'You all right, darlin'?' He squinted at her neck.

'It's only a scratch,' said Pa Bigsby. 'Fortunately.'

'That was a near one, but! Just as well Ma wasn't here.'

'Just as well,' agreed Pa. 'She will be waiting anxiously for our return so we must be on our way.'

'The cab's here waiting for you, Pa.'

'Excellent, Kieron. What a good friend you are!'

'What's happened to Blunt-Face?' cried Elfie, suddenly remembering him. In the hubbub he'd been forgotten. 'Maybe he's got away!'

Chapter Twenty:
The Man Called Blunt

But Ronald Blunt, alias Reginald Basildon-Blunt, and a few other names as it was to turn out, had not escaped the custody of the police. They had been well prepared by the inspector from Scotland Yard. When the affray had started in the street with Clinker, Blunt had emerged from the leather goods shop and attempted to run off in the opposite direction. Unfortunately for him, however, two constables had been well-placed to cope with any such emergency. They had pounced on him at once. Two further officers had entered the shop, arrested the owner and sealed off the premises.

'Our man has not got away, I am happy to report,' said the inspector in response to Elfie's question. 'Nor has his accomplice. Look behind you!'

They turned and saw the men standing on the pavement opposite, handcuffed to two uniformed policemen. Blunt was staring down at his feet.

Elfie had stopped trembling.

'Hey, you, Blunt-Face!' she shouted.

Blunt lifted his head and looked directly at her.

'Elfie,' murmured Pa Bigsby.

She knew it was supposed to be wrong to gloat but the man was wicked and deserved everything he got. Besides, the temptation was too strong and she was not as virtuous as Pa, and never would be, so she carried on. 'I hope you rot in hell for what you've done to my father! How're you going to like living behind bars? You won't be able to touch my Papa there. Scum!'

The crowd cheered and Blunt gave her a filthy look. If looks could kill, the way they said, she'd have dropped down dead on the pavement right then and there, never to rise again. But she was standing fully upright and still full of fire.

'Perhaps that will be enough now, Elfie,' said Pa Bigsby, laying a gentle hand on her arm.

'Mr Bigsby is right, dear.' Her father, though, did not sound too displeased. She thought he might have liked to have had a good go at Blunt himself but he was too well-mannered.

'Our cab is waiting,' Pa Bigsby reminded them. 'We must say goodbye to the inspector for the present.'

The inspector came over to shake their hands.

'You suffered a terrible ordeal, young lady,' he said to Elfie, 'but you bore up gallantly and you seem to have recovered remarkably well.' He touched Joe on the shoulder. 'And here is our hero.'

Joe looked embarrassed.

'You is a real true hero, Joe!' cried Elfie.

'Are,' said Pa Bigsby automatically, making both Elfie and Joe laugh. 'You do it it to get a rise out of me at times, don't you, Elfie?' He smiled.

The inspector told them that they were waiting for a Black Maria to come and take the men away. He leaned out into the street. 'Ah, I believe it is coming now!'

A large black van, with ER emblazoned on its side in honour of King Edward, was making its way down the street, powered by two strong black horses. As it parked, the crowd, which had been growing steadily, surged forward and had to be moved to the side again. The back door was opened up and Blunt and the shopkeeper were led inside. Clinker had to be carried. He was barely semi-conscious and in no state to walk. The crowd jeered and shouted insults. A couple of men threw stones and were reprimanded by the police.

'It is getting ugly now.' Pa Bigsby frowned. 'Time we were gone.'

The inspector said he would be in touch. 'I will call on you at the *Pig and Whistle* if I may?'

'We shall be at your service,' said Pa, giving him a small bow.

'What about Parker, sir?' asked Joe.

'We arrested him as soon as Blunt had left his office.

We made sure he wouldn't get wind of what was happening and try to bolt.'

'That just leaves the man from York,' said Elfie.

Chapter Twenty-one:
The Man From York

The following Wednesday afternoon they were all gathered in King's Cross station. The train from York was due in ten minutes.

'This time you must stay well back,' the inspector cautioned Elfie. 'Don't make any kind of movement at all that would attract attention.'

She nodded. He meant that she shouldn't have taken that peek at Clinker. If she hadn't, they might not have had so much trouble with him. But it had worked out all right in the end, hadn't it? This time, however, she was resolved not to put a foot wrong. Besides, she was going to have Dowdy by her side the whole time. Glued to her side, he had informed her. He was wearing his ordinary street clothes. The inspector, in full uniform as usual, would be waiting out of sight at a discreet distance, as he had put it himself.

'We must be careful about this,' he stressed. 'We don't want to frighten him off.'

Elfie nodded again.

'There will be plain-clothes policemen near the barrier. As soon as you see the man tell Constable O'Dowd and he will take care of the rest.'

'He might not come,' said Elfie.

'We're aware of that but we decided it was worth the gamble. The train appears to be on time.' The inspector glanced up at the station clock. 'Everything clear now, Constable?'

'Yes, sir,' answered Dowdy.

'Very well. Take good care of the young lady, then.'

'Oh, I will, sir. You can count on that.'

'Good. Go and take up your positions then.'

Elfie liked the idea of 'taking up their positions'. She wished they'd let girls join the police. Dowdy said they were nowhere near strong enough for the work. Joe was strong, yet he didn't think he would be allowed to join either. But no one could stop him becoming a lawyer.

They stationed themselves a few feet to the left of the barrier but near enough for Elfie to get a good view of people coming through.

'Oh, I do hope he comes, Dowdy!'

'So do I, believe you me! It'd be grand to get the whole lot of them wrapped up and behind bars.'

The arrest of Mr Reginald Basildon-Blunt had been kept quiet so that the press would not leak the story and warn off the man from York. The search of Blunt's house had revealed a collection of ivory as well as precious stones, rubies, diamonds and emeralds, and a small amount of gold. Elfie would have loved to have seen them but they had been locked away in the depths of some police vault to be used in evidence against Ronald Blunt. In Clinker's house they had found some gold bars and a goodly number of bottles of the best Napoleon brandy.

'Enough to keep them locked up for a good few years,' the inspector said.

The search of Blunt's office brought to light evidence of forgery and malpractice, involving Parker as his accomplice. In the first place, of course, Blunt had been acting illegally, as a debarred solicitor. The police had plenty of charges to bring against him.

Elfie had asked her father if everything would be all right for him now that Blunt was out of his way, but he had said no, though it was a relief, at least, to be rid of the man.

'I still have debts to settle, Elfie. Unfortunately.'

The train from York was late in the end. A constable came over to tell them.

'Points problem at Potters Bar.' He made a face. 'They're working on it.'

'I hope he doesn't jump off the train while it's stopped.' Elfie felt anxious.

'No reason why he should. Unless he suspects he's

about to walk into a trap, but I don't see how he could. There are a couple of coppers on the train.'

'But they don't know who he is, do they?'

'They've got his photo from the newspaper cutting. I know it's a bit blurred, but if a man started to run they'd be after him.'

Elfie hoped the bobbies would not be giving themselves away by wearing uniforms.

'Of course not! We're not that daft.'

Elfie continued to brood. A crook could always sniff out a copper even if he was wearing ordinary clothes. At least Blunt, Parker and Clinker were out of the way and none of them would be reported missing by anybody. The police had told Blunt's daily cleaning woman that he had gone on holiday and if Clinker disappeared off the street for a few days the locals would think he'd done a bunk or been knifed in an alleyway and his body dumped in the river. The dockers who'd been doing his nicking for him wouldn't give a fig. They'd shrug their shoulders and find a new fence. Nobody liked him. How could they?

The constable returned to announce that the points problem at Potters Bar had been resolved. The train should be in shortly. He left them to return to his own position.

'Stand still now, Elfie,' cautioned Dowdy.

She put her arms by her side and stood to attention.

'I can understand if you're feeling a bit nervous,' he said.

She wasn't feeling nervous at all, just excited. She'd been nervous when Clinker had grabbed her round the neck. No, not nervous, terrified out of her wits. She'd thought she was done for. And she might have been if Pa Bigsby hadn't been so keen on them learning to play cricket. Funny how some things worked out.

The constable came back to pay them a third visit. 'Train's just coming into the platform now. Be on your guard!'

'Remember, Elfie,' said Dowdy, 'the moment you see him let me know!'

'He's never come out first. Usually about the middle.'

'Easier to get lost in the crowd that way.'

'That's what Joe thought.'

The first passenger to come through the barrier was a man in a business suit walking smartly. After him came another and then a large family straggling along, taking its time, dropping things, stopping to pick them up and getting in people's way.

'Hurry up,' muttered Elfie. 'Get a move on.'

Some couples emerged next, husbands and wives, some arm-in-arm, followed by a woman on her own with roses on her hat that bobbed up and down. Now a shawled granny appeared on the arm of a young girl. And then came a man in a fawn mackintosh and a black bowler hat.

'That's him!' shrieked Elfie, forgetting that she was not supposed to attract attention. There was so much noise going on it could scarcely matter. The main thing was that the police now knew who their man was. Whistles could be heard blowing all over the station.

The bobbies were running, converging on their prey. He zigzagged and swung to his right, trying to avoid them, but he didn't stand a chance with half the police force in London after him. At least, that was what it looked like.

The man from York was felled. Elfie cheered.

'Come on!' Dowdy grabbed her hand. 'And let's hope we've got the right man. You've to identify him, remember? '

The inspector was there, at the centre of the circle. It opened up to let Elfie and Dowdy through.

'Well, Elfie,' said the inspector, 'is this the man you've seen in the *Euston Cocoa Rooms* with Mr Ronald Blunt, otherwise known as Mr Reginald Basildon-Blunt?'

The man lay on his back, still panting from his run. He had droopy eyelids, a birthmark on his left cheek and a small straggly goatee beard that reminded Elfie of the school inspector's.

'That's him,' she said.

'You're sure?'

'I'm sure.'

He looked up at her. '*You!*' he snarled. 'I thought you was bad news when I first seen you.'

Chapter Twenty-two: A Special Saturday Night

The *Pig and Whistle* was packed. Ma was allowing only regulars in. She had to turn newcomers away. She was very apologetic.

'It's a special do tonight, you see,' she told them. 'We're celebrating.'

They already knew that, and it was why they had come. The story of how Elfie and Joe had helped bring a criminal gang to its knees had spread far and wide throughout the borough of Stoke Newington. The telling had developed as it travelled until it came to be believed that Elfie and Joe had managed the feat on their own, without assistance from the police.

'Oral stories tend to become embroidered as they are passed around,' observed Pa Bigsby. 'It is perfectly natural.'

'The police only came in at the end,' Elfie reminded him. 'Me and Joe did the leg work.'

'Joe and I,' said Joe with a smile.

He was happy. On Monday he would be returning to work for Alfred Trelawney.

Elfie's father was giving up the chambers in Chancery Lane and moving to smaller, humbler premises near Holborn Circus. They would still be convenient for the Inns of Court but would cost much less.

He had also put the house in Hampstead on the market and, with it being a fair-sized house with many attractive features in a much sought-after area, he was confident that it would sell quickly. He was negotiating to buy a four-bedroomed house in Highbury with an extra room in the attic that would accommodate a cook-general. He had explained to Elfie that a cook-general was someone who would do the cooking, washing and ironing, and general housework. He could afford only one servant. There was a small front garden and a slightly larger one at the back but no coach house. There would be no coach to house in it anyway.

Mrs Trelawney, as was to be expected, was taking all these new changes in her life badly. Ethel was being summoned at regular intervals to bring the smelling salts. When they only had the cook-general, thought Elfie, she'd have to fetch them herself. She might be better for it instead of lying on the sofa all day.

Alfred Trelawney told Elfie that he had explained to Clarissa that he was at rock bottom and so they had no other option.

'I wouldn't call four bedrooms and a cook-general rock bottom,' Elfie said to Ma.

'To her it must seem like it. Poor woman!'

'She's not poor!'

'In her eyes she is. She's come down in the world.'

'Down in the world? Sad Sid and Mad Meg have only got the one room and a lavvy in the back yard.'

'It's all relative,' said Pa. 'It depends on what one is used to.'

'Don't be too hard on her, Elfie,' advised Ma. 'She's sticking with your father, give her that. She's not run off back to her rich parents. It must be a great relief to your father.'

Elfie knew that it was. Papa said that he didn't need Clarissa's inheritance. He would build up his business, with Joe's help and earn a living for all of them.

Papa was coming to the party with Rosalind. Mrs Trelawney had also been invited, but had sent her regrets. She was somewhat indisposed. They had not expected her to accept.

Alfred Trelawney arrived with Rosalind in a cab. Elfie and Joe, who had been hovering by the door, ran to meet them. Rosalind was excited. She looked up at the *Pig and Whistle* sign and laughed. She'd told Elfie she'd like to have a sign like that at her house but Elfie didn't think her mother would agree.

'Let's go in then!' Elfie took Rosalind by the hand.

As the door opened and the noise billowed out Rosalind became suddenly shy but, once inside, with everyone surging around her, admiring her golden ringlets and her pink flouncy dress, she was back to laughing again.

'Turn around, love,' said Florrie. 'Let's see the big bow at your back. My, you is a pretty girl!'

'Are,' murmured Elfie.

Everyone was decked out in their best. Ma was wearing her going-to-church maroon silk dress, Florrie had on a new blouse in a deep shade of rose with a high collar and leg-of-mutton sleeves, and Elfie herself wore a dress of scarlet satin decorated with emerald green ribbons. Her father had given Ma money to buy new dresses for all the girls too. He had insisted. He said he still had enough money to do that! Only just, thought Elfie.

Dowdy arrived looking very smart in his off-duty clothes and was immediately surrounded. He had to recount over and over again how Joe had bowled the lump of paving stone at the forehead of the criminal who had had Elfie in his vicelike grip and been threatening to slash her neck to ribbons. The men slapped Joe on the back and their wives blew him kisses, which embarrassed him and made Elfie and Florrie laugh. Pa declared that every boy in the land should be taught to play cricket. The world would then be a safer place.

Frankie started up on the harmonium and the singing began. Pa decided to retreat to a quiet side bar, taking with him Joe and Elfie and her father. They seated themselves on the red plush banquette.

'Well, Mr Trelawney,' said Pa Bigsby, 'I suppose we could say that all's well that ends well? Would you agree?'

'Pa likes his Shakespeare.' Joe smiled.

'Who would not?' demanded Pa.

Elfie struggled with it sometimes. She liked *Romeo and Juliet* but Pa was reading to them at the moment about a king called Richard that she wasn't so keen on. Ivy had dropped off to sleep one afternoon and Elfie had felt tempted to do the same.

'But nothing is ever quite ended, is it?' said Pa. He was in what Joe called his reflective mood.

'You are quite right, sir,' agreed Alfred Trelawney. 'Life continues and we are never sure what it might bring.'

He would be thinking about Clarissa and how she would settle into her new house. Elfie couldn't imagine her making shepherd's pie and washing the dishes on the cook-general's day off.

'I still find it amazing, Joe,' said Alfred Trelawney, 'that you managed to hit the man right in the centre of the forehead. I shiver when I think of it and what might have happened had you missed.'

So did Elfie.

Joe shrugged. 'It was nothing.'

'It was not nothing!' Elfie was indignant. 'You saved my life.'

'And troublesome as you may be at times,' said Pa Bigsby, 'I think we are all glad, on the whole, that he did.'

'Troublesome!' said Elfie. 'Me?'

'Yes, you!' said Joe and ducked his head out of her reach.

The strains of 'Cockles and Mussels' came drifting through from the main bar, mingled with the sound of chattering voices and the ring of laughter.

There was one topic of conversation. The tale of Joe and his remarkable feat would be related over and over again for many years and become a legend in its time. And outside, high above the door, as the sign swayed in the night breeze, the pig danced and smiled and played his whistle to his very own tune.

About the Author

Joan Lingard has published more than thirty books for children and thirteen for adults. *Tom and the Tree House* won the Scottish Arts Council Children's Book Award. *Tug of War* was shortlisted for the Carnegie Medal, the Federation of Children's Book Groups Award, the Lancashire Children's Book Club of the Year, and the Sheffield Book Award. *The Guilty Party* was also shortlisted for the Federation of Children's Book Groups Award. *The Eleventh Orphan*, the book that introduced Elfie to thousands of readers, was shortlisted for The Royal Mail Children's Book Award and the UK Literary Association Children's Book Award 2010.

Joan was awarded the M.B.E. in 1998. She is married with three children and five grandchildren.

Joan Lingard

The Eleventh Orphan

Everything in Elfie's life is a mystery...

The Eleventh Orphan

Mr and Mrs Bigsby of the *Pig and Whistle*
in Stoke Newington already look after ten
children. When Constable O'Dowd brings
them an eleventh orphan he found on the streets
Ma Bigsby is reluctant to take her.

But there's something about Elfie, it's the first
day of a new century and Ma loves a mystery. Just
why does Elfie possess a little watercolour of
the *Pig and Whistle*?

As the mystery unfolds, Elfie's world will
change completely.

WHAT to do ABOUT Holly

JOAN LINGARD

What to do About Holly

'Come on, Holly,' said her mother, grabbing her free hand. 'And stop dragging yer feet or you'll miss yer train.'

'I'm not wantin' to go on the train on my own.'

'Well, you'll have to, won't you? I can't take you. I've my work to go to.'

When Holly's mother puts her on the Edinburgh train, in the care of a complete stranger, who happens to be a children's author, none of them have any idea of what is going to happen.

The following weeks will be unlike anything Holly has known before; Nina and Colin Nightingale and their son Johnny live a life very different to her own. But when Johnny has a terrible accident all differences are forgotten.

". . . there's a timeless message in this poignant story of a lonely little girl who yearns for stability and love" THE DAILY MAIL

THE FILE ON
Fraulein Berg

It's hard to spot the enemy within

Joan Lingard

The File on Fraulein Berg

1944. Belfast. The war drags on. Kate, Harriet and Sally read spy stories and imagine themselves dropping over enemy lines to perform deeds of great daring.

When Fraulein Berg, a real German, arrives at their school it doesn't take them long to work out that their new teacher is a spy. Now the girls have a mission: to watch her. Follow her. Track down her every secret. Prove she is the enemy.

But the file on Fraulein Berg reveals a very different story – one that will haunt Kate for the rest of her life.

CHILDREN OF WINTER
by Berlie Doherty

Out walking, deep in the Derbyshire hills, Catherine and her family are forced to take shelter from a sudden storm in an old barn.

It all seems strangely familiar to Catherine. As the torchlight dims, shadows of the past crowd in, memories of a time hundreds of years ago, when three children took refuge in a barn, not from a storm, but from a terrible plague . . .

This gripping and haunting adventure is inspired by the true story of the village of Eyam which in 1665 cut itself off from the rest of Derbyshire, so that no other village would catch the Plague.

"Vividly and sensitively realised" GUARDIAN

RAVEN BOY
by Pippa Goodhart

Legend has it that if the ravens leave the Tower of London, monarch and kingdom will fall.

London 1666, the Great Plague rages and the city is a dangerous place. Young Nick Truelove blames his King, Charles II, and vows revenge.

Inspired by the cunning of a young raven, Nick bluffs his way into the centre of the King's power, the Tower of London itself.

But, as a remarkable friendship grows up between boy and raven, a new danger engulfs the city. Nick's view of the world and his King is about to be changed for ever.

"This fast-moving adventure is rich with historical detail" GUARDIAN

You can find out more about other
exciting Catnip books by visiting:

www.catnippublishing.co.uk